# Dying Hard at The Classic

**A Lemon Boy Mystery**

By Rod Sanford

Copyright © 2018 RBS Worldwide LLC

All rights reserved.

ISBN:
ISBN-13: 9781727353167

## AUTHORS NOTE

This story takes place in the great city of Atlanta. Readers will recognize some familiar landmarks throughout the book. Some have been altered to facilitate good story telling. Atlanta natives will also notice locations that are fictitious. They are used to serve the needs of the author.

This is a work of fiction. Any resemblance between occurrences in this book and real life are totally coincidental and unintended by the author.

## Chapter One

Shawn Butterfield ran north on Atlanta's Centennial Olympic Park Drive, between the Fountain of Rings and the Sky View Ferris Wheel. He was home for one day from Birmingham A&M University, a ninety-minute drive, two hours by bus.

He was taking Saturday nights after games to go home more and more lately, most times to see family and some for times like this. He had not gone home first. He jumped on the MARTA train near the bus terminal and got off at the CNN/Stadium Station. Instead of coming up through the stadium tunnel and emerging on the International Plaza Fairgrounds, he went in the opposite direction, traversing the underground parking lot near the station and heading east on Elliot Avenue. He made a pickup at the Elliott Street Café and Bar, as he had done several times before. It was automatic. From Elliott, he turned left on Mitchell. He increased his stride as Mitchell crossed Ted Turner Drive and Ted Turner Drive crossed Marietta, which put him at the park.

He was in his black and gold Under Armor Swyft Outrun jogging pants and long-sleeve neoprene t-shirt and HOVR Phantom running shoes. He had his INOV Racing Vest Pack, the one that fit between his shoulders, packed with only the few essentials he needed for the next two days. He planned to be back in class by Monday afternoon and band practice after that.

Butta remembered prowling the area as a junior in high school after working his blocks down in the south end of Atlanta. He had been out way more than he should have been, and he was looking for trouble.

Now he was over that. He was in shape, his body lean and clean of weed, pills, alcohol, and red meat. He was getting an education, a junior at a celebrated HBU, which had so thoroughly embraced him that he had the courage to discover and then pursue his passion for music production.

He was performing every week as one of the three drum majors for the Birmingham A&M Marching Pride. When he was on the field with the power of the band behind him, he felt invincible. It was a high he could barely control.

He felt that way on nights like this. He could run five miles without stopping at a nine-minute-per-mile pace. Powerfully and proudly jogging down the streets that he had skulked through four years earlier made him feel reborn.

Even at midnight, he felt no trepidation. He was a member of the Pride, a powerful male lion moving through the urban jungle.

*Mustafa ain't got a thing on me*, he thought, laughing to himself as he increased his stride against the uphill incline of the sidewalk of Centennial Olympic Park Drive near the southern tip of the park. There were few people out at this time, but the pavement was dotted with construction pylons. Butta moved through them with a stutter-step motion that did not slow him down.

"Energy," the song by Drake, started in his wireless earpieces. It was one of his favorites. It took his mind off his breathing or the pounding of his feet. He moved north on the mission of the night.

*******************************************

"Let's stay alert out there," warned a voice over the MDT and radio unit in Officer David Cooley's squad car. It was from another officer in the other squad car patrolling this area. He thought it was McGill. David had been with the Atlanta City Police Department for two years, assigned to Boulevard Precinct. However, he had been moved around several zones every few months or so, providing backup for short staffs, vacations, and maternity leaves throughout the department.

Tonight, he was patrolling the CNN Precinct, riding backup to the officers assigned to the area around Centennial Park. David enjoyed being an officer, but he was getting annoyed with the temporary assignments. This one was no different.

As he sat in his patrol car, 21222, on Baker Avenue, next to the Georgia Aquarium, he followed the chatter of the other officers. Sam Takeshi was his partner for the shift and another temporary assignment from Precinct Two. Sam, the son of a Japanese commercial angler in Savannah and an Italian Southern belle, was a five-year veteran. He was small in stature but very fit from years in the gym. He was a sports guy, ready to discuss Falcons, Hawks, Braves, or Bulldogs.

James McGill and Nick Brody were in the other squad car and permanently assigned to the CNN Precinct. McGill was also a police union representative and very helpful. He had met David and Sam with hearty handshakes and jokes. He was African-American, medium-brown complexion, about five foot ten, mid-thirties, and average build.

Nick Brody was tall, also in his thirties, about six foot four and slim. He was a brooder, carrying a perpetual frown on his bony face, and his head was covered with thinning blonde hair. He didn't say much outside of warning David and Sam of the recent criminal activity in the area around the park.

James and Nick were stationed on the south end of Centennial Park in unit 39011. At the end of the day, they were all professional and seemed to work well as a group.

"Heads up, 21222. Possible suspect running north on Centennial Park Drive towards your position," the voice on the radio said. Now David was sure it was McGill.

"Roger that, Car 39011. Any suspicious behavior?" he asked.

"He's hauling it, carrying something in his hands. Shiny. Also a backpack. Subject matches a description from the shift briefing," McGill answered.

David was trying to remember what he had read from the briefing at the beginning of the shift. Some robberies and snatch and grabs after midnight in the area of the park.

"Subject has turned northwest and is traversing the park at Luckie Street!"

"In what direction, 39011?" Takeshi asked.

"Still heading north to your position. Picking up speed."

"Is anyone chasing him?" David asked. "Has there been a call into the station from this location? Robbery? Assault? Anything?"

There was no answer. Takeshi repeated the question.

Then he was there. David saw an African-American male, early twenties by his fitness and physique. He was in full stride, wearing black jogging clothes and white and gold tennis shoes. David watched as he appeared from the central opening at the north end of the park, adjacent to Baker Street.

"There he is!" Takeshi shouted as they watched the guy streak across their vision, heading north across Baker Street. He didn't seem to notice the police car. He continued at full stride into the Pemberton Place green space between the Georgia Aquarium and the Coca-Cola Museum.

"I'll go after him on foot," Sam said, opening his door and getting out onto the street. "Cooley, you drive around to the north end of the aquarium and cut him off in case he makes it the next cross street!"

Sam jumped out of the car and started to run. He noticed David was still just sitting behind the wheel.

"Go, man!" he shouted. Then he chased after the running man. David heard him shouting at the runner but could not make out exactly what he was saying.

Finally, David shifted into drive, hit the roof flashers, and sped west. He decided against the siren. No sense raising the calm when they didn't know what or whom they were pursuing.

He took the right at Centennial Park West and pushed north up Luckie Street NW, a flashing blur past the Legal Seafood Restaurant. The streets were empty save for a few shadowed bodies moving up and down the block. No one was shouting for police or chasing a lone subject.

At Ivan Allen Boulevard, he turned right and slowed, a parking garage to his right. The runner should be coming from the direction of the parking garage. The SweetSpot Nightclub was on the other side of the street, opposite the direction of the runner. The SweetSpot music was loud, and the house was full. Ivan Allen Boulevard was full of people just in front of the club.

Whoever the guy was in the backpack, David needed to address it before he got to Ivan Allen Boulevard and the street full of Friday night partiers.

"Takeshi, I'm in position. What's your twenty?" he asked into the radio.

No answer.

"Unit 39011, what's your twenty?" he asked

"We've moved into position on Baker Street, south of you in case he circles back," McGill said.

"Still in pursuit!" Takeshi shouted into the radio, his breathing heavy. "He's coming up between the museum and TGA! I think he's wearing headphones; he can't hear my commands to stop."

"Somebody fire a warning shot!" McGill shouted over the radio. "We got to get his attention!"

David eased forward, pulling just east of the nightclub. The idea was not to draw any more attention to himself. Thinking this through, he concluded the subject couldn't hear anyone yelling at him. It would have to be a visual thing.

He put the patrol vehicle in park, got out, and moved swiftly without running. He continued about a half-block east, away from the nightclub and parking garage. He was at the opening to the green space between the Coca-Cola Museum and the Georgia Aquarium. He was standing just west of the Center for Human and Civil Rights.

At first, he saw nothing, just darkness. Then he heard it. Rhythmic steps, light but definitely footsteps. They seemed to be coming from different directions, a lone sound bouncing off the walls between the museum, the aquarium, and the sidewalk. When the runner did appear, he was a moving shadow; then the reflective gold trim of the jogging suit in full stride became clear. He was about fifty yards away. David looked for Takeshi, who should have been chasing the runner, but he couldn't see him.

He waved and yelled, but the runner didn't seem to see him. He seemed to be looking in a different direction. Just like that, the runner changed his course. Instead of running directly towards David, he moved more northeast, to David's left. If David didn't do something, he was going to lose him.

He began running straight east along Ivan Allen Boulevard to try to cut the runner off before he reached the street. Beyond was a honeycomb of condominiums and townhomes. He would be much harder to track in there.

From the corner of his eye to the right, he finally saw

Takeshi. He was out of breath and not moving very fast. He appeared to have his service pistol in his hand. David remembered the plan to fire a warning shot to get the runner's attention.

As David continued to run east, it became obvious the subject was in better running shape than all of them. The ground on the east side of the Center for Human and Civil Rights sloped down toward the street. There was also a set of steps on that side. David could clearly see the runner headed that way. He was in the zone. David could see the sound buds in his ear. He would not reach the runner before he descended the steps and reached the east end of Ivan Allen Boulevard.

Just as they were parallel to each other, David stopped, pulled his gun, and planted his stance.

■■■■■■■■■■■■■■■■■■■■■■■■■■■■■■■■■■■■■■■■■■■■■■■■■■■■■


Butta had decided to cut between the museum and the aquarium to save some time and avoid any more traffic lights and construction on Centennial Park Drive. There were plastic silhouettes of ghost and goblins hanging from the trees and the sides of the buildings. Halloween was a couple of weeks away.

He was running late, but the bus into town had been slow. Squeezing his right hand over the package, he focused on the task. Being late, he knew they would be mad, but once he made his delivery, things would be just fine. There were few streetlights between the two buildings, but he was a member of the Pride, and this was his lair, his savannah.

The song "DNA," by Kendrick Lamar, started in his earpiece, and Butta expanded his stride with new wind.

This run could only be described as "sweet." His wind was so much better, and running in the fall was much better than the summer in Atlanta or Birmingham. There was a breeze created by the tunnels of skyscrapers in the downtown area. It felt good against his face. It smelled of exhaust and the cheap fast food he had given up two years ago.

He could make out the lights at the SweetSpot Nightclub through a spread of trees just before reaching Ivan Allen Boulevard. A few more steps, and he would be through to the street. Then he would cut east again towards his original path.

He had the nagging feeling that he was being followed, but he chalked it up to running with headphones. In the past, he would spend too much time constantly looking over his shoulder, losing his pace and tripping over his feet. He was already late.

*A member of the Pride does not get distracted. Stayed focused. Eyes forward*, he told himself as he came up the east side of the Center for Human and Civil Rights. He hit the steps one at a time, feeling powerful with each toe tap.

Emerging from the last stand of trees, he could now see the people out in front of the SweetSpot, to his left and west of where he was going. They were milling around, doing what people do at the club. He could not hear them; his ears were full of "Slippery," by Migos and Gucci Mane. He imagined them like people all over the city, letting off steam, talking to girls, drinking more than they could afford, and forgetting real life for a few hours. Butta felt an irrational sense of smug superiority to them at that moment.

About three feet from the sidewalk, he noticed the lone figure running east on a line straight for him, and it was a white man, a cop, and he had his gun out.

*What the hell is this?* Butta thought as he continued to run out of involuntary impulse. Then his felt a mighty punch in his chest that stopped his music and lifted him off his feet.

## Chapter Two

The next several hours were a slow nightmare for Officer David Cooley. From the second he saw the runner fall back as if he'd run into an invisible wall to the scream he let out as he hit the ground and then to the crimson pool that oozed from under and all around him – David felt as if he were living in another person's reality.

In his mind, he heard his voice screaming, "I fired into the sky! My piece was pointed to the sky."

Maybe there was a ricochet from a tree? If so, he hoped the injury was not so bad. But there was so much blood. The runner, a kid actually, was unconscious. David could not revive him. He called his backup, but no one was near. *Where the hell are they? Takeshi should have been right behind me.*

David had called for an ambulance and backup. Maybe they could find Takeshi, Brody, and McGill.

By the time his partners did show up, David was surrounded by SweetSpot partiers, half of whom were recording his attempts to revive the subject on their cell phones. His tardy partners dispersed the crowd amongst grumbles of protest. David heard the names Eric Garner, Michael Brown, and Eric Harris more than once.

In a few minutes, the ambulance was speeding away with the unresponsive young African-American runner in the back. They didn't want to further endanger him, so they didn't search him for identification.

Afterward, David was interviewed in the back of his squad car by the shift lieutenant and assistant chief of detectives. By the ninth time he repeated the story, it began to sound fairly ridiculous. A warning shot? Who does that outside of the movies?

It had been suggested in the heat of battle, and he'd been chasing the kid for reasons not quite clear. *Brody mentioned the briefing notes, and we all just got in line. We just wanted to stop the kid and question what he was doing running through the park at midnight. There had been robberies and assaults in this area in the last few days.*

"Cooley, we need your piece," McGill said, standing outside the squad car. He had a sympathetic expression. It was the first time David had spoken with any of the other three since the ambulance had arrived. He unhooked his holster and handed it through the window. McGill was wearing latex gloves. He deftly took the Glock and placed it in a clear evidence bag.

"For what it's worth, Cooley, I believe you," McGill said. "It had to be some kind of accident, a ricochet or something. The guy didn't look that bad when they took him away."

"You think?" David asked.

"Naw, and hey! We still don't know what he was doing running through the park at midnight."

"You're right," David said flatly.

"A lot of unknowns at this point," McGill said, and he tapped the top of the car door. "Go home. Get some sleep."

------

David lived in the Glenwood Park area of East Atlanta in a rental owned by his wife's father. Anousha Baldwin-Cooley was a debutante daughter of one of the largest African-American agents of the State Farm Insurance Company. In addition to writing a large percentage of policies within the Interstate 285 circle, he also held substantial commercial property holdings, such as the corner stucco post-modern single-story where David lay awake that night.

David had come home to find Anousha in her knee-length pajama shirt but still awake. She hadn't heard, but she just knew something wasn't right. She was slim, about five ten with natural braids that came to her waist. She was a caramel-colored woman with high cheekbones and bright brown eyes. Her long legs were curled beneath her as she handstitched a glittery green piece of chiffon fabric. It was to be a princess Halloween costume for their daughter, Daria.

"Anousha, I swear by all my sanity that I shot straight up in the air," he said after explaining what had happened that night for what seemed like for the hundredth time in the last six hours. "I just don't understand what happened."

"Could there have been another shot, from one of the other officers?" she asked.

"No, he was shot from the front; all the others were to his rear," David said, staring up at the ceiling.

"What about another shooter; you said it was suspicious, a kid running through the park at midnight. Just like you drove around the block to cut him off. Maybe whoever he was running from did the same and shot him."

"As much as that sounds plausible, how did that phantom chaser shoot at the exact same time that I did?"

"And where exactly was he when you fired your warning round?"

"I told you, just at the opening between the museum and the aquarium."

"And there was no other sound from there?"

"At midnight? Of course not."

"Where did all the people come from? The ones recording you?"

"The nightclub on the other side of the street. When I fired, they all got more interested in that than the loud music . . ."

"So, there was other noise on the street," Anousha said.

David tried to think back to the level of sound from the SweetSpot. Could it have been loud enough to hide a second shot? David wasn't sure. Either from confusion or utter fatigue, he eventually slipped into some level of sleep.

Nightmares kept him tossing and turning for the next four hours, until his cell phone vibrated. It was his commanding officer. The runner, a one Shawn J. Butterfield, had died on the operating room table two hours ago. David was to report to police headquarters at the Public Safety Headquarters by

11 am, in about two hours.

Chapter Three

**Red Kitchen and Bar, Downtown St. Louis, Missouri**

I sat in my usual corner in the Red Kitchen and Bar in the lobby of the Hyatt on the riverfront. It was an open-air deal with a bar just off the lobby. There was a row of booths and about fifteen four-person tables. The head chef was an old school friend named Curtis Bennett.

When we'd been scouts, Curtis had been the only member of our troop who could cook, and he'd kept our city asses from starving on camping trips. Judging from the popularity of the breakfast buffet at Red Kitchen, he hadn't lost his touch.

I liked being in a place where I wasn't likely to be known. Red Kitchen was a tourist spot, specifically for those staying at the Hyatt.

I wasn't much of a morning person, but business happened in the morning, so I got up in the morning. I sat at a back table near the restrooms. The server, a beautiful but scowling woman wearing a perpetual frown, told me, "Lemon Boy, I wish you would move to a booth. You too big for this little table."

My name is Darryl Phillips, also known around St. Louis as

Lemon Boy. The nickname was a carryover from my childhood days in the streets of East St. Louis, Illinois. My friends and enemies thought my light brown complexion, light freckles, and gray-green eyes worthy of a title of ridicule. Even after growing to six feet and two hundred pounds, the name just stuck. My partners and I ran a security outfit called Paladin.

The last few years had been tough but profitable. There had been the chaperone assignment of St. Louis teenagers to Colorado for the Nubian Winter Festival that had turned into a crime event involving gold fever. The year before that we'd been protecting my ex-girlfriend, the eighties pop diva Lola Montclaire, during the New Orleans Jazz Revival. Both events had garnered national headlines. As a result, Paladin Security had all the work we could handle.

My partners, Teri Lovejoy, Bobby Farr Sr., and Bobby Farr Jr., and I were hiring extra security on a daily basis to cover all the work that came our way. We were covering events from New York, Miami, Houston, and Los Angeles. The proverbial "they" were calling us Nubian Security, the firm to contact if you were having an African-American cultural event.

The ex-cop in me felt strange about the notoriety. The business owner in me felt any press is good press.

Not expecting to meet with anyone this morning, I was shocked when my mother, Verna Phillips, seventy-three, walked into the lobby. She was dressed in her business jeans that fit like slacks and a silk floral blouse with flared sleeves. Several years ago, she had made her peace with hair extensions and given up her trademark curly wigs, and now she sported black braids with some gray here and there. She was flanked by a set of twins, male, African-American, in their early twenties. I knew them well – Chunky and Choppy Wells.

"Good morning, Darryl. You got a minute to talk a bit of business?" she asked as she sat at one of the chairs. The twins stood behind her with solemn faces. I was wondering when or if I'd told my mother this was my morning spot. Sometimes, she was a better detective than Bobby and me.

Chunky and Choppy Wells had been small kids in my neighborhood when I'd been in high school. I'd watched them grow into mischievous adolescents, clumsy, awkward, and funny teenagers, and now serious young adults. It was still hard for me to take them seriously.

"Can I get you something, Mama?" I asked.

"No thanks," she answered. She was in full business mode, no familiarity. Verna Phillips was very warm as mothers go, but she would not be deflected from her objective once she was set on something. She also never passed up an opportunity to teach "young folks" a lesson in how to get things done. At forty plus, I still counted as young folks.

It was obvious that the twins were in Verna Phillips's class. I motioned for the twins to rest their feet.

"You been watching the news?" she stated more than asked. She placed a folded copy of the *St. Louis Post-Dispatch* on the table between us. I took a look at the article that had been highlighted in yellow.

"Investigation continues in police shooting of HBU drum

major," I read aloud. This story was in heavy rotation on television, radio, and newspaper. It also had a sad, familiar feel.

Weeks before he was scheduled to perform in the Big Boo Halloween Classic in Atlanta, an unarmed African-American male had been fatally wounded by a white police officer in the blackest city in America. The deceased, Shawn Butterfield, had been a drum major with the Marching Pride of Birmingham A&M University.

There had been equal calls to boycott and attend the BBH Classic.

Protesters wanted a collective to eclipse the Million Man March. Counter-protesters wanted to match them in number. Everyone was demanding justice from the city prosecutor and the police department.

"This shooting of our boys has to stop," Mama explained in clipped tones. "The Ferguson Force for Change intends to go down to support the cause."

"Sounds like a plan," I said patiently as I sipped my grande latte.

"We need Paladin to provide security for the protest march," she said flatly.

"Security against what?" I asked between sips, as if I didn't see what was coming.

"The police? Counter-protesters? You know what can happen when a bunch of people get together."

"I do," I said, putting my cup down. "I don't know if it's a job for us."

"Why not," my mother said, indignation forming at the corner of her words.

"It's too big; it would be too big for any security crew. Tens of thousands of people stretched across blocks. What's your budget?"

"For what?"

"Security. How much can the Ferguson Force for Change afford to pay?"

"We thought you would want to be a part of this movement. You're from the St. Louis area. You see what they are doing to the young black men of this country. . ."

"So you want Paladin to incur costs to go down to Atlanta and provide security for the FFC against who knows whom, for who knows how long, and do all this for free?"

"Not exactly, Lem," Choppy Wells said, raising his hand like in school. He was three inches shorter than his brother and thirty pounds lighter, but he did most of the talking. Those were the two ways to tell them apart: height and weight. They were identical in the face.

"How exactly?" I asked.

"The way we figure it, you could, like, put your people in the crowd and help stop anything you see. Maybe be a credible witness in case of an incident. Maybe—"

"I get it," I said, holding my hand up. "You want imbedded witnesses. People who see things and document what they see. But you don't need security to do that. I can teach your people what to do to protect themselves and how to document what happens. That won't cost you anything, and it's better than having assigned security."

"How so?" my mother asked, still not buying it.

"Mama, you can't have enough security to catch everything everywhere. Protests stretch across blocks and involve various groups all doing different things. Anything that happens where we are not will be lost. If we teach people how to protest defensively, they catch everything that happens."

"But what if you had a client, someone you were protecting at the event?" Mama asked.

"A paying client? That would be different. Still not sure how much help we could give, but we could give something, I guess. I'd have to talk it over with Teri and the Bobbys."

The table was silent for a few seconds. Chunky whispered into the ear of Choppy, who said, "There's also moves being made by the police and the prosecutor to clear the officer."

"Of course," I said matter-of-factly. "What are they saying? And how do you know this?"

"The white officer, David Cooley, swears he shot in the air and not at Butta. One theory is there was another shooter there at the same time."

"That's weak," I said. I picked up the newspaper and scanned the story. "Do they talk about ballistics?"

"Huh?" Choppy asked.

"Have the autopsy results been reported to the public? Did they recover the bullet from the body?" I asked, remembering I was talking to civilians.

"I don't think so, but would they make something like that public?"

"They will if there is enough public pressure."

"Well, that is something Paladin can help with, seeing as how you all are ex-cops," Choppy explained. "Like you did out in Colorado?"

It was becoming clear to me what they were asking. They knew we couldn't provide security for a protest rally. That was just a cover to get my crew down there to privately investigate.

"Let me get this straight," I said, smiling over my morning cup. "You want me to snoop around like Alex Cross or Matlock and get evidence to help put away that white officer?"

"Who's Matlock?" Chunky asked.

"You want Paladin to snoop around like a real-life A-Team and save the day."

Blank expressions from the twins.

"Never mind," I said. "Look, the answer is no. First, I don't have the access or the right. Second, even if I could, it wouldn't do you any good. That is not how investigations work. Not the kind that stand up in court."

"Are you sure this isn't because you used to be on the

force?" my mother asked, always trying to push my buttons.

"No, if Cooley broke the law, I would be the first in line to support his prosecution. It's about poking your nose in other jurisdictions when I don't even have a jurisdiction. Not anymore. I'm private."

"Yeah, but you got to the bottom of what happened in New Orleans with that singer," Choppy said.

"That was different; she was my client, and she was killed on my watch."

I still winced at that thought of the late Alexis LaVette.

"Well, since you can't or won't travel with these kids, then you CAN work with them to give them some things to keep them safe before they head down there."

I promised my mother I would. I also promised the twins that Teri Lovejoy and I would meet with them personally before they left for Atlanta. The twins weren't happy, but they seemed mollified for the moment. Mama asked them to give us some privacy. She handed them twenty dollars each, and they scurried for the coffee bar.

Afterward, Mama and I talked about personal things.

Her health? She had been managing multiple sclerosis for a few years now. Hence the addition of the cane. Since her diagnosis, she had thrown herself into the conversion of my childhood home into the Phillips Senior Citizens Center she had started and maintained on a shoestring budget from donations and state grants.

Even with that, she kept enough energy and time to stay in

my business.

"Have you spoken to Lola?" she asked.

"No," I said flatly.

"Have you tried?"

"Yes."

"You leave a message?"

"Yes, and before you ask, Mama, I told her I was sorry about how things went down when she told me about TruLuv."

"Why don't you call your son by his real name?" she asked.

"Because, at this stage, he prefers to be called TruLuv, and I'm going to respect that. Says he's not sure if he's going to keep that name."

"Yeah," she said and sipped her tea while reflecting on what I'd said. "I know I give you a hard time on some things. But that was some tough news for you to take. A son you meet for the first time as an adult?"

"It was," I said, looking out the front lobby windows of the Hyatt. The sun was reflecting off the Mississippi River, making the surface a rolling white. I watched those rolls for several seconds, until my involuntary anger about this situation subsided.

"But remember, TruLuv found out about his mother in the same way and at the same time."

"I talk to TruLuv all the time. At least once every couple of weeks. We're Facebook friends, Instagram followers, and

Twitter buddies."

"Good, but what about Lola? What about his mama?" my mother asked.

"I have no idea," I said, staring at the light on the river again.

"Shame, just a shame," she said to no one in particular.

"A shame of her making," I said, giving in to the edge of anger so keen I could taste it on my tongue.

"True. Very true."

I mentally rolled my eyes. Mama never outright agreed with me unless there was a "but" coming after it.

"But right or wrong, someone needs to be the glue that brings you three together finally," she said. "Did you hear the song TruLuv made for me?"


I nodded.

Allen Parrish, aka MC TruLuv, my son, had released a new album a month before. He was the new incarnation of rapper: independent, inclusive, intelligent, and cool but with a nerdish flare.

In the last eighteen months, he and I had found out that he was my son and that my ex-girlfriend Lola Montclaire was his mother and not his aunt. He had been born about seven months after she and I had broken up. Just before her big break, which had launched her into late-eighties superstardom. She'd had the baby and turned him over to his aunts on her father's side from New Orleans. They'd rehearsed and played out a story about his mother dying and his father not being available for over twenty years.

I wondered, *Damn, why can't the daddy be dead or some other noble reason? Why do we always have to be deadbeat deserters? Even in a lie. The rest of the story was so elaborate.* I continued to take deep breaths.

For most of his life, TruLuv had known Lola as his famous Aunt Lola, until a series of life events and my partner Teri Lovejoy had forced her to come clean to him and me. Teri had pulled on some instincts and vague clues until she'd figured it out. I was even mad at her for a while, although I do not know why.

The present status of all this was a clumsy but sincere relationship between TruLuv and me, but neither of us had summoned the capacity or ability to work our way back to Lola.

My mother got to her feet. She pretended to be studying the jewel-studded top of her cane.

"You three seem like lone souls drifting apart in the same swimming pool. All of you very successful but lonely human beings. If one of you could just open up and extend your heart to her long enough to see there is something to salvage here."

"Well, I tried," I said quickly, and the look she shot back at me let me know I should have stayed quiet.

"Don't tell me you tried, Darryl," she snapped and bumped her cane on the floor one time. Her eyes flashed with real venom and then softened almost as fast.

"Listen, don't ever say that to someone who has lost someone to death. A person who would kill to have the chance that you ignore every day. The chance to speak to the love of your life one more time."

There it was. The lesson of the day for me from my mother. My father had been gone almost fifteen years, a victim of a highway fatality on I-70, but there was not one day she didn't miss him down to her core. I produced the proper tone of silence, taking in what she said.

She turned as if to leave but then turned back to me. "Just one question?" she said, pointing her cane at me. I nodded.

"Do you still want her? Before you found out about TruLuv, you two were well on your way. Like old times."

"I don't know," I said.

"Try me again," she said, stomping her cane, sending another echoey "kack" through Red Kitchen.

"Yes, Mama, I guess I do, but it still hurts," I confessed, hating that I was breaking my cool pose, my façade, in the middle this public place.

My mother nodded as if in deep thought. No one affected me like Verna Phillips.

She nodded her thanks, gave me the smile that let me know that I'd gotten the lesson, waved the cane playfully, and strolled out of the Hyatt.

## Chapter Four

KeeVon Sherman had been the starting quarterback for the Birmingham A&M Fighting Lions for two seasons, but starting the first Saturday in September, he was the hottest topic in all college football circles.

On that Saturday, the Fighting Lions were served up as the opening victims of the powerhouse Division I University of Virginia. The Cavaliers were ranked three in the nation.

It was customary for large football programs to schedule smaller opponents like HBU schools as their first or second game of the season. The larger school could work out their rough edges without any conceivable chance of incurring a loss. The smaller school would realize a sizable financial advantage and maybe a highlight or two.

This usually worked flawlessly.

Until that day in September.

On that day, the Fighting Lions of Birmingham A&M marched proudly into Charlottesville to play with their heads high. At the end of the day, the score was Fighting Lions 35, Cavaliers 6. The "Goliath" school had been crushed by the "David" team from the HBU East Conference.

However, the true story of the game was KeeVon, who led the team to a record 552 yards of total offense. He threw for three touchdowns; he also ran for 210 yards.

In the next three games against HBU conference opponents, KeeVon continued on what the media called his Sherman Death March. Birmingham A&M outscored their opponents 130 to 22. KeeVon had already thrown for 1350 yards and scored 23 touchdowns either throwing or running.

He was the surprise of the season. No one in sports journalism knew what to do with him. He was also a social media phenomenon because of the hurdles, dives, flips, and good looks that seemed to be made for video streaming.

Rappers, country music performers, and reality television stars followed him on Instagram and tweeted about his moves, his smile, his light-brown eyes, and his perfect six-pack abs. His YouTube channel was trending so strongly that the NCAA and Birmingham A&M discussed whether his videos were a monetary infraction of his eligibility.

ESPN analysts even floated the idea of his inclusion in Heisman Trophy discussions.

In interviews, he was soft-spoken, shy, and intelligent. He could afford to be sweet with a mother like Madina Riley-Sherman.

Madina was a force of nature. KeeVon's father, Bernard, a captain in the US Army, had died before KeeVon's tenth birthday from a combat ambush in Kandahar.

Since then, Madina had only one objective: to create the kind of man her husband would have created had he lived. God, grace, and grades were non-negotiable. Also courage. It was the brand she was building for him: the 3Gs.

"We don't beat our chest, but we don't back down," she was

often quoted as saying. The "we" was not euphemistic. It was literal.

When high school and college coaches and counselors tried to water down his classes so he could focus on football, she didn't back down. When the large schools offered scholarships if he moved to wide receiver, she didn't back down, and when they wanted him to close all his social media, citing NCAA eligibility violations, she put her Florida A&M University law degree to work representing her son in the arbitration hearing that ruled in their favor.

And it was Madina Riley-Sherman who approached the athletic departments for Birmingham A&M and their arch rival Banneker College about making their annual game a new football classic.

Both schools were lukewarm about the short notice: six weeks to design, set up, and sell ads for a new football classic. Then she brought in her secret weapon.

The event manager of the ATL Dome in Atlanta was a law school classmate and her dead husband's fraternity brother. The NFL Atlanta Falcons were on their bye week during Halloween weekend. The dome was available.

When they floated the idea to advertisers, a chance to see the Sherman March, the man who had dismantled the University of Virginia, the David who had slain Goliath, it was a no-brainer, and the Big Boo Halloween Classic was born.

This morning, KeeVon and his mother were meeting with Charles Bullock, event manager of the dome, Richard Gettis, athletic director for Birmingham A&M, Lily O'Neal from Banneker College, Renita Roundtree from the mayor's office, and Captain Terry Sayles from the local police department.

"Ticket sales continue to be active," Charles said. "I think we have some special musical talent for everyone. A number of old-school acts headlined by Lola Montclaire, who is selling out on her comeback tour. We are working on getting additional acts from ATL records, who produced the Big Boo Classic theme song. Also, we have female Drum Major . . . or is it majorette?"

They all turned to the young lady sitting quietly on the sofa.

"Drum major – Gina Pombo," she said, sitting confidently.

"Uh, yes, Ms. Pombo is a two-year member of the Marching Pride. She will take the place of Shawn Butterfield. She will be the first female drum major to perform for Birmingham A&M," Richard explained proudly.

"Great," Madina stated with a smile. "Pombo? You an island girl?"

"Correct, mon," Gina affirmed, slipping into perfect patois. "Mi people dem come from St. Ann Jamaica, fi true."

"Yeah," Madina said, smiling and nodding. "This will be good national exposure. This is the year of female empowerment and the Me Too Movement. The press will like it."

"You as good as Butta?" KeeVon asked doubtfully.

"I got a rhythmic death march of my own, Mr. Sherman," Gina said, giving all but a finger snap in her attitude and crooked grin. She never altered her relaxed sprawl on the sofa.

Even the grown folks in the room let out a low, "Oooooooo."

"Ha, I like her," Madina said. "Keep that swagger, young lady. You gonna need it on that field. A lot of guys might have a problem with a female drum major, but there will be just as many of us rooting you on. We all owe the late Mr. Butterfield our best."

"What about press?" Renita asked.

"We got sessions set up for KeeVon that shouldn't impact his practice."

"You mean like today," KeeVon said. "It's a weekday; my team is in Birmingham, and I'm two hours away."

"We know, K," Madina said. "But I wanted you to be a part of this meeting."

"Ok, Mama, but why?"

Madina turned to the rest of the men in the room.

"Uh, KeeVon, we want to talk about your interviews, especially in relation to certain subjects." This was from Richard Gettis from Birmingham A&M.

"Ok," KeeVon said impatiently.

The older men in the room hemmed and hawed a bit. Then Charles, her mother's law school buddy, spoke up. "Kee, we suspect you will get some questions about the shooting of Shawn, the drum major "

"Good, because I have some definite opinions about that," KeeVon said, finally showing some interest.

"Yes, we know," Charles said. "That's why we want to talk to you. We need you to package your message."

"Package my message?" KeeVon asked.

"Package your message," Lily said.

"What the hell, Charles" Madina said already frustrated. She leaped out of her seat and knelt in front of KeeVon's chair, like she'd done when he'd been a small child.

"KeeVon, what you put on your blog about the shooting? That was good stuff."

"Thanks, Mama," he said.

"But it was also pretty raw," she added.

"I just spoke my mind," he said confidently. "Like you taught me. If we believe it, we don't back down."

"Yeah, that's true," Madina said. KeeVon noticed she had a tentative look on her face. It reminded him of the days when they had lived in a one-bedroom apartment after his father had died and they'd had to sell their house. The look on his mother's face right now reminded him of the times back then, before she'd gotten her degree and started practicing law. He wanted to make that look go away.

"What is it, Mama?" he asked.

"Well, it's just this?" Madina said but then faltered.

"No shorts, Mama," KeeVon said sternly.

It was the phrase Madina had taught him. It was his father's phrase. No shorts meant just speak plainly, no beating around the bush looking for shortcuts. It was how Bernard Sherman lived his life – and how he wanted his son to live.

"We need to have your future tweets and blog posts reviewed before you post," she explained, her expression stern.

"Reviewed? By who?" KeeVon asked.

"Me," Madina responded. "And Charles, Richard, and Lily."

"Really?" KeeVon said, his surprise palpable as he rose from his chair.

"We got a lot riding on this ballgame," Richard said. "The sponsors are a little nervous with the shooting and the city already on edge. They don't want anything to cause tensions to boil over into a riot."

"A riot? Because of something I posted?" KeeVon said to the entire room. "Maybe the people are rioting because yet another murder has been committed by the police."

"Yes, see, its statements like those that worry the sponsors," Charles said.

"Fine, let them pull their sponsorship," KeeVon snapped. "I won't be silenced just for some advertising hush money. If people with access don't speak up, then who will?"

The entire room was silent for a few seconds and full of fearful looks. Except for Madina.

"You want to have your say?" she asked.

"Of course, Mama," KeeVon said plaintively.

"Then shouldn't it be factual? I mean, only fools pass off erroneous information as fact."

"Right?"

"Ok, then all we are asking is to check the factual quality of your information so we don't look foolish. So we don't tarnish your brand."

"I just don't understand why now."

"Because you're busy. You already worried about missing practice. Then there is your schoolwork. You don't have time to check what you write."

"But most of the time, I'm just expressing how I feel; no harm in that," KeeVon said.

"It is if you feel differently later," Madina responded.

"Then I can post that?"

"And you come off looking like a wishy-washy kid, an all-brawn, no-brains jock? In the meantime, all those people who follow you and take your feelings as their own, who take your advice to heart, what about them?"

KeeVon was thinking about her words.

"Then there is your future; what we are doing this for?" Madina continued. "Nothing, and I mean nothing, gets in the way of our ultimate goal. Do you remember what that is?"

"Yes, Mama," KeeVon said sulkily.

"What is it? I want to hear it come from you so all these important people in this room can hear it."

KeeVon felt a little sheepish, but he recited it like he did in his prayers, his meditations, and during his marathon workouts.

"My ultimate goal is to achieve a first-round draft selection to the National Football League, to walk across that stage as a college graduate, and to represent my family and my race and the 3G Brand with dignity. In the name of Jesus, amen."

There was a collective sigh around the room.

There was a knock on the door. Charles's secretary walked in with a sheet of paper and whispered in his ear. He read it and looked stunned. After a few seconds, he instructed her to "Show 'em in."

Then, to the rest of the group, he said, "We all need to stay here for this."

A few seconds later, the secretary ushered in Jack Fontone from the governor's office and another man, white, over six feet tall with rugged outdoorsman looks stuffed in a dark single-breasted suit. He was a walking billboard for law enforcement.

"Hello, everyone. I'm Purvis Conners with the Department of Homeland Security," he said to the stunned room.

Everyone else introduced themselves. Conners seemed no-nonsense. He didn't mince words or dwell on pleasantries. It wasn't personal to him. It was his job.

"The notice you have in your hand notifies all organizing parties of the Big Boo Halloween Classic that the Department of Homeland Security will be installing security around the venue."

He said the name of the event with heavy emphasis on the "B's". KeeVon thought it sounded like a disrespect on some level.

"Ok, but I don't understand," Charles said. "Have there been threats against the classic? A terrorist threat?"

"No," Conners said. "But there may be against some of your guests. You see?"

He paused and reached into his jacket pocket. He pulled out another sheet, folded along its length. He handed it to the mayor's representative. She read it and handed it to Charles on her right.

"The president is coming to the classic?" Charles asked, as if he could not believe what he'd read. The rest of the people in the room gathered around the paper he still held in his hand.

"Not exactly," Connors said. "The president wants to make a statement about gun violence. With the recent incident, he wants to make sure all sides are heard."

"Oh my God," Madina said. "He wants to side with the counter-protesters?"

"The president campaigned as a devout protector of the Second Amendment. He sees Atlanta as a perfect forum for debate and for all to express themselves according to the First Amendment."

"Where does he plan to rally?" Renita asked.

"Well, as he sees it, ATL Stadium Fairgrounds are open to everyone, even the president."

"Wait, that's where the classic activities are being held, hundreds of vendors, children's attractions," Madina said.

"Yep, and where most of the protest against firearms and the Atlanta Police Department will occur. The president just wants both sides to be heard," Connors explained, both his hands held up to show no threat.

"But we have the fairgrounds booked for the entire weekend," Richard explained.

"Yes, you do as a gift from the city and state. You were not charged any fees for its use," Connors said. He had done his homework.

"Because it was going to make a lot of money for them," Madina said.

"Well, with all due respect, Ms. Sherman, I think the president can sell just as many hot dogs as young KeeVon, if not more," he said with a courteous nod in KeeVon's direction. "And since use of the grounds was a gift and no cash exchanged hands, well . . ."

The room was silent.

"Don't worry; we've already gone over the layout. We won't need to displace any of your vendors. We will use quite of bit of the parking, however."

"This can't be happening," Lily said.

"Oh, yes it is," Connors said as he headed for the door.

"We've even notified the sponsors, who look to get a lot out of this weekend. They couldn't be more excited."

Connors waved a loose salute to the room and left. Jack followed him out.

The room was quiet for almost a minute. Then it descended into a cacophony of voices all talking over one another.

David Jeremiah Travis had been elected forty-fifth president of the United States in a campaign described as part show business, part bullying bluster. In the end, the people had voted, and one of the narrowest margins in presidential election history had elected him.

For the last year, he had been true to his more notorious words. He'd attacked immigration rights and reversed executive orders that protected unions, workers' rights, personal freedoms, and the environment.

Now he had turned his sights on the Big Boo Classic. He was going to crash "the Biggest Halloween Party on the Gridiron."

Madina and Charles worried there would be new calls for boycotts. Captain Sayles worried if there was going to be enough police available. Renita thought about a call to request the National Guard. The athletic directors were already on the phone to their respective schools and their coaches to control the message and student reaction. KeeVon couldn't wait to get back to school and practice. He wanted to play this game more than ever. He would have a statement but at the proper time.

## Chapter Five

Marques Campbell Butterfield sat in the back of his black 2008 Lincoln Town Car with the word "Camp" on the license plate. It was the vehicle he drove to visit family. He thought it was more inconspicuous than his other imported whips, which ranged from champagne white to flaming magenta.

He was working up the nerve to go see his Aunt Rita. Her son, and Camp's favorite cousin, Butta, had been gunned down seventy-two hours ago. Butta had been like a little brother to Camp, and he had been proud of what Butta had been doing in school and with the band. Even after all his college success, Butta had still hero-worshipped Camp, a street dealer, a thug, who should have been on that coroner's table instead of his young cousin. Butta had still dressed like Camp. He'd been wearing the Under Armor premium gear that Camp wore while conducting business. Camp still wondered if it had been a case of mistaken identity.

Camp had police on his payroll. Had they gotten tired of the payoffs and tried to destroy him? He couldn't wrap his mind around that. The payoffs were good. Very good. Also, why would they think he would be running through Centennial Park at midnight? No, they knew who Butta was. So, why hadn't the protection kept him alive?

Maybe it was a rival. The area north of where Butta had been shot belonged to an underground gambler named Dancing Disciple Daniels. Daniels ran illegal gambling and prostitution in the blocks just past those apartments on the other side of the SweetSpot Nightclub.

However, Daniels was in a different line of business. He didn't move horse, tar, or weed. He would have tried to get in Butta's pockets, overextend him on credit to get to Camp, maybe even using intermediaries to kidnap Butta. Killing connected people in cold blood was not his way.

When Camp had found out about the shooting, he'd tried to strap up and go find that fucking cop. He'd wanted to start a war on the police department. He had been restrained, as always, by his right-hand person, Cadillac Kai Davis.

He and Kai had come up in the game together since about tenth grade. She was African-American and Japanese, and therefore, she'd caught it from all sides. She was not Japanese enough for one side. She was not black enough for the other side.

Camp had befriended her because she was tough and had no loyalties established like all the rest of the thugs in his neighborhood.

Over ten years later, they were still the only ones the other could trust. Kai was the one who sobered him up after day two and rode with him to go see his aunt by day three.

They were sitting in the car in front of Aunt Rita's house on Metropolitan Avenue, just east of Flat Shoals Southeast. Camp was the older image of Butta, five foot ten, slim build, and medium-brown skin. He had a round face with hooded eyes that he kept on watch like he was perpetually looking for something or somebody. He wore his hair in a short fade that stayed trimmed and had a thin goatee.

Kai was five three and wore her hair in jet-black, shoulder-length cornrow braids. Her coloring was somewhere between beige and the color of raw peanuts. She had an angular face that gave you the impression of a feral woodland creature. She didn't smile a lot and many times spoke with her hand over her mouth, an old habit from childhood teasing of her unusually large teeth. However, she was ferociously loyal to Camp Butterfield. There were at least three missing teeth, one finger, and the tip of one ear from unfortunate individuals who'd had the misfortune of bad-mouthing Camp or planning to do him harm and she'd gotten wind of it.

"I can't help but think this got something to do with me," Camp said, looking out the window at his aunt's house. He could still see Butta sitting on the porch, like he always did when Camp would roll up to see him. Their fathers were first cousins; both had died in a trucking accident along Interstate 20 between Monroe, Louisiana, and Dallas, Texas.

He had taken Butta with him everywhere, the barber shop, the suit man who sold merchandise out of his van, the shoe store where all the latest sneaks were for sale, and all his girlfriends' apartments. Butta had been good luck for him and had given him something legit in which to believe. Something to make all the dirt he did worth doing. Butta had been his only attachment to normality in an otherwise insane criminal existence.

Camp knocked on the door, Kai at his back. They both wore black jeans and short black jackets with white mock neck shirts.

Rita Butterfield opened the door slowly and just stared at them.

"Aunt Rita, I am so sorry; I meant to come sooner but—"

"Don't," Aunt Rita said, holding up a hand. "Don't compound your disrespect with lies. Come in if you coming."

Camp stepped inside, and Aunt Rita put a hand up to Kai. "I invited my nephew into my home," she explained in a clipped tone. "His junkyard dog can stay outside, please."

Kai held her hands up and stepped back onto the porch. Aunt Rita slammed the door in Kai's face.

She and Camp sat on the sofa in the front living room. Kai could see them through the front window.

"Auntie, are the police telling you anything?" Camp asked to start the conversation.

She shook her head and took a sip of what looked like tea.

"I just want you to know I will do whatever I can to get answers. I have lawyers and people in this town that owe me favors. Important people."

"I'm sure you do, Marques," she said, looking into her cup.

"Butta was my brother."

It was quiet for about a minute. Camp felt the need to fill the air with words, but Aunt Rita was not for it.

"Tell me something," she said. "Are these important people going to bring Shawn back to life?"

Camp had the sense not to answer.

"You going to kill that cop that shot my baby?" she asked.

"Auntie, I—"

"Yes or no, Marques?" Aunt Rita asked in earnest. "You are a big man. You sold your soul to the devil and sell poison to your own people. What good is all that if you can't do something as simple as kill a man who killed your 'brother,' as you say?"

"Aunt, I promise you I—"

"Boy, shut your thug ass up. You couldn't even work up enough courage to pay your respects for three days."

"I . . . I . . ."

"Three days ago. They told me my baby was killed by another bigot cop. I have been so full of rage and hopelessness that I'm exhausted. Lord, forgive me, but I want that motherfucker dead."

"I hear you," Camp said, his head down.

"Do you, Marques? Because I saw it clearly in my head. I wished for you, Shawn's brother, to do what he does. Unleash the wrath of hell, and I would find that dirty dog hung from a tree or shot in the head or something. Then day one and day two passed, and nothing."

Aunt Rita stood and walked around the room.

"What kind of world is this when the police can gun down a kid like Shawn, and our mad dogs won't even step up and do what they are good at doing?"

"I'm sorry," Camp mumbled. He didn't know whether to be remorseful or shocked at the words coming out of his sweet Aunt Rita.

"Sorry? Sorry for what, Marques? You weren't sorry when you broke your mother's heart and dropped out of school and started selling that junk. You weren't sorry when you set yourself up as the gang kingpin for Fulton County. You not sorry for slowly and systematically killing your own kind, one rock at a time. Now, when you can actually do something to help your family? Do what you have worked soooo hard to become – a cold-blooded killer? NOW you say you're sorry."

The room stayed silent for several minutes save for Aunt Rita's sobs. During that time, Camp felt more helpless than he ever had. He questioned himself about why he hadn't acted, why he hadn't stepped up true to his reputation. That fucking cop should have been dead.

"I got to know one thing," Aunt Rita said. She was standing at the fireplace mantle, across the room from where Camp sat. She looked small and frail. "And don't lie to me. Did they kill my baby because of you? Was this about your business?"

"I don't know, Auntie, but I will find out."

Aunt Rita nodded. "He looked up to you. He wanted to be a success to make me proud, but also to make you proud."

"I know. I was always proud of him," Camp said.

Aunt Rita's face started to break into another sob. Camp wanted to go to her, but she wouldn't have it.

"You find out. Do that for your cousin, for your brother. I want to know why my baby was killed, and if it has to do with your business, then handle your business."

"Yes, ma'am," Camp answered solemnly.

"Promise me!" she shouted suddenly, tears streaming down her face.

Camp stood and rushed over to his aunt. At that point, she let him hold her.

"I promise, Auntie. I won't let you down," he said, holding her tight.

"Don't let me down," she said, sobbing. "Don't let Shawn down."

"I won't. On my life, I won't."

They stayed in that embrace by the fireplace for almost ten minutes, neither of them talking. Camp's mind was already plotting how he was going to put that cop in the ground, sending a message to the whole police force that this shit wouldn't be tolerated.

Kai was waiting for him when he stepped outside.

"How did it go?" he asked.

"She's broken, CK," Camp said as they walked back to the Lincoln. They got in and signaled the driver to go. "But we gonna start to mend that."

"Meaning. . ."

"Meaning I'm out to do what you stopped me from doing

three days ago. Now that cop is gonna be hard to get to, but I'll get to him."

"Yeah about that. . ."

"No bounties or contracts, man. I don't need gun-happy niggas fucking this up. We taking him out personally."

"So, yeah, um . . ."

"What's wrong now? You too soft to pull a trigger now?" Camp asked. He knew the last thing to do was question Kai's intestinal fortitude, but he was ready to go to work and needed his "ride or die" with him.

She continued to look worried, and Camp knew it was bad. Kai never looked worried.

"What is it?"

"I been doing research on that cop, his background, and his people in case we need to squeeze family members. Some of my calls just came back."

"Yeah, okay," Camp said, his voice strong, not betraying the trepidation he was feeling.

"I looked up his immediate family. The guy does work in the black community."

"So. . ."

"Camp, he don't seem like no redneck. He got awards for his service to Big Brothers Big Sisters and shit like that. The internet is full of videos of him playing, working, and helping little black boys and girls."

"Ok, but he still made the wrong mistake. I don't care what his virtues are; he'll get his reward when I send his ass to heaven."

"Right, well, it's about his family. We just need to think through this."

"What, nigga? What are you not telling me?" Camp said. "I ain't in the mood for riddles!"

"It's his wife," Kai said, rubbing her face.

"Is he married to someone famous, someone connected?"

"It's Nousha," Kai blurted out.

"What?"

"You heard me. His wife is Nousha. Your Nousha."

Camp stared at his second in command, saying nothing. He couldn't believe how complex this was getting. Kia continued her report.

"They got married three years ago, and . . ."

"Three years ago?" Camp said, almost shouting. "I was fucking with her a year ago."

"Fifteen months, to be exact," Kai corrected. "You didn't know she was married?"

"Hell no," Camp said, rubbing his face like someone trying to remember an event. "Um . . . she said she was seeing someone else but that it was going badly."

"Well, couldn't have been all bad. They got a kid," Kai said.

"A kid?!" Camp pulled his hand from his face. "CK, wait . . . how old?"

"Calm down; the kid's four years old," she assured him as she worked her phone. "See, here's a picture."

Camp looked at the picture on the screen of the phone of David Cooley in a family portrait with the sexy, smoky, but secretive woman that he knew as his Nousha. There was a small female child sitting in her lap. She looked like a café-au-lait version of her mother. Maybe she had her father's eyes. Nousha's beautiful brown face held a smile he had never seen her make. Her hair was still in braids, but they were worn down. Her hair had always been up when they'd been together, exposing that long, soft neck. She seemed out of place in this domestic scene, but obviously, his experience was the anomalous exception.

Kai motioned for Camp to continue flipping through the pictures of Officer Cooley posing with disadvantaged youth of all backgrounds and races and getting awards from the mayor's office and local church federations.

"This doesn't make sense," Camp said. "This cop ain't what I thought he was. You think he found out about Nousha and me? And decided to take out Butta?"

Kai just shook her head. "It's too many variables. How did Cooley know your cousin was going to be at that part of town at that particular time of night?" she asked. "You didn't even know he was in town. I still think we need to think this through. Feels like there is a long game at play here. I don't know if we are the final mark or just casualties in the way. But before we start pulling triggers, we got to know all the pieces on the board."

Kai was right. His cousin had been killed by the cop married to his ex? It was too set. Like a bad movie plot.

"Ok, let's keep digging, but secretly. Just you and me. We continue to act vengeful, like we want the blood of that cop. We show that to our contacts on the street and our connects on the police force."

## Chapter Six

"You made the decision without talking to us?" Teri Lovejoy said. She was in her mood of righteous indignation. We were at the office for Paladin. The company had started in my duplex home. However, thanks to our recent success and expanding business needs, we'd moved into a spot on South Grand just across from Tower Grove Park. Teri, Bobby Farr Sr., Bobby Farr Jr., and I met here every day at 10 AM.

Bobby Farr Sr. and I had been partners in the St. Louis Police Department. After a bad bust against some powerful people that had put Bobby Farr Sr. in a wheelchair with paralysis below the waist, we had been forced off of the police force. We'd started Paladin a few months later.

Bobby Sr. was in his mid-fifties, but you wouldn't know it by his almost perfect physique above the waist. The tough Southside St. Louis son of Dutch and Irish parents would not let non-functioning legs keep him from working, from competing, from living. He was in the gym at 5 AM every day. He had a fifty-two-inch chest and massive biceps, all muscle. He had that square jawline and a ruddy face with the most stunning set of blue eyes you ever saw on a man.

Bobby Farr Jr. looked more like his mother. He was six foot four and muscular in that youthful way without being bulky. He wore his brown hair cut short on the sides and full on top. He'd been an All-American tight end, but he'd blown out his knee during his second year playing college football. His hardworking father had wanted him to continue his education. However, the equally headstrong son had wanted to join the business world.

Teri Lovejoy was my prodigy on the force and work little sister. She was five foot three inches, with a PhD in clinical psychology. Her family was part of the black intelligentsia, and her great-grandparents had been on the early boards of the Urban League and the Southern Christian Leadership Conference. Despite all that, she wanted to be where the action was. When she left the police force and joined Paladin, her parents didn't speak to her for six months. After I assured them I would keep her alive, they came around.

We were the base of Paladin Security. We specialized in security at public events and for human clients such as celebrities and political figures. We keep a list of independent security muscle in fifteen major cities that we brought on as we need them.

This morning, Teri had found out about my mother's request for us to assist the Ferguson Force for Change. I wasn't sure how, but I was certain my mother had made a call to her as soon as she'd left the coffee house.

"Lem was right to turn it down; we can't provide any kind of security for something like that," Bobby Sr. said.

"It's not about that, and Lem knows what I'm talking about," Teri said. She was pacing just a bit. I could feel one of her "black power" talks coming on.

"Yeah, Pop," Bobby Jr. said. "It's about standing with your people. St. Louis is still reeling from this crazy cop behavior. Some things are bigger than money."

Bobby Jr. was cute the way he was always ready to pick up

the banner for Teri's causes. I didn't know if it was a big sister worship or a jungle fever crush.

"Shut up, boy," Bobby Sr. snapped back. "I haven't seen you in one protest rally. Now you are Robert James Farr Jr., friend to his soul brothers in need."

"Don't make fun, old man," Teri said. "Bobby Jr. is right. None of this is going get better if you fogeys keep your heads in the sand. We got to support these other cities facing the same problem. Help them organize."

"And we will help; I told my mother and the twins we would help them with some strategy, but we got a business to run," I explained.

"You also said you would consider it if we had a client at the Big Boo Classic, right?" Teri asked.

"That's right," I said vaguely, remembering the question during my mother's hard pitch this morning.

There was a knock on the outer office door. Teri walked over and opened it. Allen Parrish, aka MC TruLuv, my son, walked in with a wide smile.

"Did someone call for the client?" he said cheerfully.

Feeling like I had been bamboozled and that my own words were being used against me, all I could do was sit there, smile, and let things unfold.

TruLuv was that new generation of hip hop artist a la Lupe Fiasco, Kendrick Lamar, and Chance the Rapper. He was rhythmic, soulful, higher conscious, but he still got booties out the seats. He obviously got that from his mother. I could not hold a tune with a suitcase.

In his late twenties now, TruLuv was about six feet, with an average build, fit but not muscular. If he had been in my generation and living on my block, his physical shape would have been called "poor" by the old folks sitting on the porch. However, he was in show business, and that skinny look was money in the bank. He wasn't my complexion, nor did he have his mother's mahogany brown skin color. Instead, he was somewhere in the middle, with a handsome adult face, a constant smile, and brown eyes that seemed very attentive.

It was easy to be proud to call him my son. However, I still struggled to see a likeness, although Teri said she saw the similarities more in the mannerisms than the looks. Teri was the one who had discovered the secret in New Orleans a couple of years ago and confronted Lola. She'd given Lola a chance to tell us the truth, or she would. My protégé sister got on my nerves at times like now, but she always had my back.

TruLuv worked the room: hugs and kisses for Teri, dap handshakes with Bobby Jr., a salute and bow to the unsentimental Bobby Sr., and a quick one-armed hug for me. That was only the second time that had happened.

"TruLuv is joining the billing at the Big Boo Halloween Classic. He is on the halftime show in front of the Marching Pride Band," Teri explained.

"When did this happen?" I asked. "I checked the website this morning. You were not on it."

"Just happened today," he explained, standing there with a

confidence common in true entertainers. "My friend's label Peachtree Sounds produced the theme song. I plan to put my touch on it, plus a few other songs."

"And they just put you on the billing at this late date?" Bobby Sr. said suspiciously.

"He's MC TruLuv, Pop," Bobby Jr. said. "Who wouldn't want him on the stage?"

"Well, thank you, son of mine," Bobby Sr. bantered back in their typical sardonic Irish patter. "I would have never guessed that had you not just enlightened me."

"It was easy, Mr. Farr," TruLuv said, plopping down on a couch in the conference room. "I agreed to do it for free."

"Free?" we all said at the same time. TruLuv held up one hand and punched on his phone with the other. In a few seconds, he turned the screen to the rest of us in the room. "I started a GoFundMe page. I asked people who want to see me at the classic to send twenty dollars to my fund. The entire fund will go to the Atlanta Movement for Change and to the family of Shawn Butterfield."

"That is smart, bro," Bobby Farr Jr. said.

"I agree," I said, truly moved by the generosity and his creativity.

"So, we're on, Darryl," Teri said enthusiastically. She refused to call me by my nickname. "For the classic?"

I hesitantly looked at TruLuv and then back to Bobby Sr., who shrugged one massive shoulder.

"You told Mother Phillips you would do it if we had a client," Teri pushed.

"I say we vote," Bobby Jr. said, already holding his hand up.

"No, no, we don't need to vote," I responded in a conceding tone. "Teri, start the paperwork. Bobby Jr., get the gear ready. We're gonna drive to Atlanta."

The two scurried out to their offices like teenagers, both high-fiving TruLuv as they left.

"I'll start making contacts with the local police, letting them know we will be in the area working," Bobby Sr. said as he began rolling his iBOT chair for the door.

"Thanks," I said, still thinking.

"All our Atlanta assets may be engaged by other firms. We're coming into this game late."

"I know," I answered. "If that's the case, check Louisville and Nashville. We can pick them up on the way."

Bobby Sr. waved a hand, signifying that he had heard me as he rounded the corner, his chair deftly quiet. I got up from my chair, walked over the door of the conference room, and closed it.

"I need to talk to you," I said to TruLuv, who was still sitting on the couch, laser-focused on something in his phone. He was enlightened for his age. He paused whatever it was he was doing and looked up at me, smiling, which made me smile.

I sat on the sofa next to him. We exchanged a few

pleasantries about his music, his next tour, my work, our health, and his newly minted lovable but meddling and manipulating grandmother.

"Ok, Tru," I said, using a portion of his stage name. I had tried calling him by his given name, Allen, but it just seemed off to both of us. "We need to discuss some things about this trip. Your grandmother wants me to do more than just security."

"I know," he answered matter-of-factly. "I don't want that."

I sighed with relief.

"I plan to do the snooping myself," he responded confidently.

"Wait, Tru, that's—"

"I got some things in place. We will get to the bottom of this."

"Wait. What do you have in place? Who are you talking about?"

"I just need you to watch my back while I'm there."

"That is crazy," I said and instantly regretted my tone. "How are you going to check out anything? You're a celebrity. And who are these people you are talking about, and how do you know you can trust them?"

"Lem, it will be alright. Those things we pursue in righteousness will also come with his protection."

"That protection being me and my team?" I asked. "That's a little presumptuous, ain't it?

"Maybe, but I don't think you are as against this as Grandma thinks you are. This is another one of those cases that can make a difference in all those that come afterwards. The opposition is waiting for us to wear down, but we won't wear down. People like me have to use this celebrity for more than just selling music or likes and clicks. We have to be a voice for the generation."

"I get it. Being a voice is one thing, but poking into a murder and police business is another," I explained.

"I want to show you something," he said and began tapping on his phone again. Then he held it out so I could watch a video.

It was a street scene, at night. There were many people in the foreground, mulling around. Then, in the background to the left, I saw and heard a muzzle flash and then someone fell to the ground. The video was grainy and shot at night. It was on a loop, so when it restarted, I stared in the general area of the muzzle flash.

"This is video from the SweetSpot Nightclub camera facing the street. It was taken in as evidence."

"How did you get a copy?" I asked, watching the video loop repeatedly.

"I told you; I got people that I trust, that want to see justice done."

"Ok, so I don't know what this proves. I see the cop, Cooley, running; he stops and appears to shoot, but it was too dark to see in what direction. Not sure whose side this helps."

"Yeah, but Butta goes down almost immediately; it must

have been a ricochet or a direct shot."

"But you said the police have this evidence," I reminded him.

"True, but the question is, will they use it," he answered. "This will be one piece of evidence out of many that they won't be able to deny."

He was right. The video was compelling but not conclusive. I continued to watch the shot on the phone screen. It was dark and grainy; a good defense attorney could refute it in court. I had to admit to myself that the theory of a ricochet from a shot over Butta's head landing at mid-chest seemed a bit off.

But this was police work, based on facts and what could be proven beyond a reasonable doubt. I guess I had been quiet too long. TruLuv felt I needed more convincing.

"Lem, this the personal," he said. "I met Shawn two years ago, when I conducted a music mentor program with the Big Brothers of Atlanta. He was talented. Raw. Decent on keyboard and guitar with practically no training. Just playing by ear."

"A musician as well?" I asked.

"Yeah. If you worked as many hours as I have to perfect just one instrument, you recognize it when you see it. But he was also just as interested in hanging in the streets, smoking weed, and imitating his older cousin."

"Who is his cousin?"

"Camp Butterfield was, and is, the biggest drug dealer in Fulton County. Shawn dressed like him and, at the time, wanted to be just like him."

"Until you turned him around?" I asked, half believing.

"Maybe a little, but I think it was when he saw he could be something else. Really saw it. Then he was easy to teach. He sought me out, as opposed to the other way around. I got him the audition with Birmingham A&M. My frat brother is on the staff there."

"I have to ask," I stated. "Are you sure he didn't slip back into the life. Take back up with his cousin?"

"No way," TruLuv said, shaking his head emphatically. "He was making straight A's. He worked out like a fiend – a rock-solid core. AND! He gave up meat."

"Are you sure," I asked. "They thought he was carrying a weapon, something shiny."

"I know," TruLuv snapped back. "It turned out to be a twelve-inch hoagie from Elliot's Café just south of the park."

"Oh my God," I said more to myself. The story was sounding like one told too many times in the past.

"And that makes no sense. I know for a fact that boy hadn't eaten meat in over a year."

"Are you sure?" I asked.

TruLuv tapped hurriedly on his phone again. In a couple of seconds, he showed me an article about the reformed drum major that had been run in the Birmingham A&M school newspaper. The article made several references to his meatless diet and how it had improved everything from his endurance to his mental acuity. Members of the band even called him "Butta Lettuce," an ode to his plant-based diet.

"That kid would not be eating an Italian hoagie," TruLuv said with conviction. "You think it was a put there by the police?"

"No," I said, thinking. "If they were going to plant something at the scene, they would have just made it a gun."

TruLuv nodded.

"But if I was the uniform on this case, that would be a thorn I would want to file down. Let me see the video again," I asked.

I watched but could not tell. It was too dark. "He certainly sounds like he was living right. You got any idea where he was going? Obviously not home. His mother lives in another part of town," I said, remembering information from the news story.

"No, but I wish I did. I've asked some of his bandmates. They said he was going home more and more on Saturday nights after daytime home games, but they assumed he was just going to his mother's house."

"Well, he was headed somewhere to see someone. What else is in that part of town?"

TruLuv tapped on the phone for a few seconds. Soon, he had a GPS satellite view of the area near the SweetSpot Nightclub.

"Ok, he was shot about here." I pointed out the area indicated in the newspaper article. "Continuing north would take you into that area of apartments and condos."

"He could've been going there to see someone," TruLuv said. "Could we canvass the area? That's what it's called –

canvassing?"

"Yes, but slow down," I answered. "Why is that important? You are sure this officer Cooley shot him?"

"I have seen how these things go. I want to close down all the reasonable doubt. There's even some black people on Cooley's side."

"Really?"

"Yeah, he's got a long record of working with disadvantaged youths. Got a black wife too. Plus a lot of people know Shawn's notorious uncle and figured he was back in the family business."

"This is a mess, Tru," I explained. "We got to proceed carefully on this. You want answers, but you aren't exactly invisible."

"I know."

"And this is a police matter . . ."

"I know."

"And what if folks are right and he was rolling dirty?"

"He wasn't, Lem. I know it."

"Then there is his cousin. If he is what they say he is, then he has people on the street digging into this just like you."

The room was silent. TruLuv didn't have an "I know" for that one.

"I see you are determined to do this, so I'm going to help, if for no reason other than to keep you safe. If you get your narrow ass killed, your grandmother will kill me."

We both laughed at that, so I thought it was a good time to ask.

"I see your mother is performing; you gonna reach out?" I asked.

"I . . . I don't know, man," he said, his charismatic façade breaking for the first time since he'd come into the office.

"You gonna be on the same stage; how do you avoid her?"

"We're performing different nights." He shrugged with a sheepish smile.

"But what about when you do, 'Speak Your Mind'? Who's going to do your parts on each other's version of the song?"

"What was she going to do before I signed on?" TruLuv blurted back, aggravation tinging his words.

I backed off, holding my hands up to show my stepping off of his emotional corns.

"What about you, Lem? You weren't taking her calls."

"We haven't talked, but I'm reaching out," I mumbled.

"Well, let me know how that comes out," TruLuv said with more than a little defiance. "Although you should know that from what my aunties in New Orleans told me, she had just about written you off."

"Well, I wouldn't blame her," I said, trying not to show the panic I was feeling.

"So, what's the point?" he asked.

"Two points," I said. "One is that your really cool grandmother wants us to try. You know how it is to be on her good side, but you don't want to know the other side."

That made him laugh. "And the second point?" he asked.

"The most obvious one. It's in your name. Love."

## Chapter Seven

Lola Montclaire and her band were at rehearsal inside the ATL Dome, going over the sound check. They were usually very jovial, laughing, joking, and eventually getting the work done. Today was quiet, solemn, and full of mistakes and retakes. The whole team seemed off.

Lola was a true working diva. She'd come up in the mid to late eighties and had a twelve-year run, with hits like "Speak Your Mind," a high-powered dance song that still got mixed into everything from karaoke song lists to exercise mixtapes and even Muzak. By 2000, Lola had allowed herself to slip into obscurity, needing a rest from the limelight and touring. She survived a private fight with cancer and began mentoring younger artists.

Then, in 2012, a lesser-known rapper by the name of MC TruLuv covered a hip hop version of "Speak Your Mind" and convinced Lola to sing the hook without sampling. It was an easy sell, as TruLuv was her nephew. What they didn't realize was the song was the catapult launch of his career and the resurgence of hers.

In the midst of their new success and through a series of revelations, she was forced to confess to him that she was his mother, a child she'd had just as her career had been taking off.

The response was nuclear. A loving and creative family relationship became cold, barren, and strained. It affected their work. Lola's meteoric comeback continued to burn hot, but it all seemed hollow without her nephew/son to share it.

She also re-lost the relationship with me.

We had been high school sweethearts and had gotten back together in New Orleans two years ago. Then she'd told me that TruLuv was my son. More atomic fallout.

It had been her fault. She'd made the decisions over twenty years ago for success and fame. Now she was paying the price. She had tried to give us both time to digest the shocking news, but it was pushing past a year now. That time in New Orleans, where she'd had both men she loved the most in her life, had been wonderful.

"Is this how divas rehearse?" a woman's voice said sarcastically from just offstage.

Lola snapped out of her thoughts and whipped her head around.

"AAAAiiiiiiiiii!" she shouted. "Get your skinny ass up here!"

"Good thing I am skinny; not much room on a stage these days with you. Not sure which is bigger, your ego or that beautiful bubble ass of yours."

"Fuck you, shrieking cow!" Lola said, laughing and holding her arms out as if to hug.

"You wish," Thomasina Brown said as she came up the stage steps from the audience gallery. She was dressed in white dress slacks, tube top, and sheer blouse.

They hugged each other tightly, turning in the middle of the stage.

Thomasina and Lola had been two hungry backup singers in

the early 1980s with dreams of making it big. Lola was from St. Louis, with a style of R&B and dance music, trying to become the next Grace Jones or Chaka Kahn. Thomasina was Los Angeles pop and big ballads, trying to become the next Cyndi Lauper or Debbie Harry.

They'd risen up the charts at the same time as the new voices of the late eighties and early nineties. When Lola's "Speak Your Mind" hit number one on the R&B and dance charts, Thomasina, renamed Tommi B, hit number one on the pop charts with "Muscle Love," which became a mainstay on pop radio, the aerobic exercise scene, and in gay bars from San Francisco to New York.

The two of them didn't rest on their laurels, going from friends with obscure careers to fiercely competitive superstars. Las Vegas ran betting lines for which of them would win the most Grammy Awards. Designers waited in line to design their clothes and stage costumes. Their tours ran simultaneously as each tried to outdo the other in attendees and revenue. They had regular cameos on television shows and sang on soundtracks for major motion pictures.

Through all of it, they remained friends, never forgetting the old days when they had shared everything from Slim Fast shakes to high-heel sandals. They kept each other grounded from the heady days of fame. While others burned out on booze, drugs, and the grind of the work, these two had lived long enough to enjoy the comeback resurgence they were experiencing today.

"What are you doing here?" Lola said breathily after they'd excused themselves to one of the dressing rooms.

"Same as you; I'm singing. During the president's visit," Tommi B explained.

"What the hell? I thought he was going to speak and leave?"

"Nooo, he is planning an entire rally. Gonna campaign for some local candidates. There's gonna be a speech by the National Brotherhood of Police. Then there is me as the closeout act."

"You know it's on the same fairgrounds as the classic?" Lola said pensively.

"I just figured that out; that's why I'm here," Tommi B confessed. "My greedy manager signed me up for the gig before we realized what the president was trying to do. Now my name is going to take a hit for aligning myself with 'the president.'"

"So, just pull out," Lola suggested. "It's not like you need the money."

"Not that simple," Tommi B explained. "These people have long memories, bad tempers, and a lot of influence. They've more than implied that if I back out now, I could be in trouble with my sponsors. I might even have trouble booking venues in tour cities."

Lola felt the fear for her friend. They both had learned that career resurgence was great. You were smarter, your voice was more seasoned, and you had a built-in generation of fans. It was a dream come true. However, you were always looking over your shoulder for the cold water of reality to wake you up with the new hot talent always pushing up from below. It was better to be thought a demanding diva than to truly act it out with promoters, local radio stations, and the fans. Tommi B pulling out of the concert days prior for whatever reason would be interpreted as such. The president's people would make sure of that. Even claiming illness or exhaustion wouldn't work. People would just say, "See? We told you she was too old to perform!"

## Chapter Eight

Anousha and David Cooley sat in the living room, holding hands. They were listening to the lawyer sitting across from them. It was Ben Kagen from the Police Union. McGill was there as well. He was the union representative.

"It's still early in the investigation. Internal Affairs is moving very slow on this one to make sure they got things right the first time," he explained.

"The shiny thing he was holding turned out to be the sandwich from Elliot's Cafe," McGill said. "Did you think it was a gun?"

"Of course not," David Cooley said for what felt like the hundredth time. "I was aiming in the air, not at him. McGill and Brody suggested a warning shot because the kid had on headphones."

"While we are waiting, there is one thing out there," the lawyer announced. "The DA is offering a deal."

"A deal?" Anousha asked, puzzled. "Has he been charged with anything? Arraigned?"

"No, but depending on how things go and the court of public sentiment, and—"

"We're not discussing any deals on a prosecution that hasn't happened," she snapped back, clutching David's hand.

"Anousha, we can hear him out," David said. "He's obligated to tell me as my lawyer, right?"

"True," Ben said. "The offer is three to five years for reckless discharge of a firearm."

"Jail time?" Anousha asked. "No way."

"Well, we do have a dead young man in the morgue. We couldn't expect a slap on the wrist for that. They promise David would serve in a protected facility for law enforcement personnel and white-collar criminals. With good behavior, he could serve eighteen to twenty-four months inside and the rest on home arrest."

David was silent. It was one of the thousand times in the last few days it had dawned on him that he would actually go to jail. When he thought about the young black man dead in the morgue, he didn't see how this would end any way other than him going to prison.

The more he thought about his explanation of a mistaken ricochet bullet, the weaker it sounded even to his own ears. That wouldn't be enough to satisfy justice, his family, or the public. David even admitted to himself that if he were Shawn Butterfield's family, he would want more.

"To hell with that," McGill was saying as David came back to the present. "Cooley, keep your head up; we are going to get to the bottom of this. We got officers scouring the trees to show that ricochet."

"Do we know where he was going at that time of night, running through the park?" Anousha asked tentatively.

"No clue," McGill said, "but it was something illegal. You know who his cousin is?"

David had no clue, but Anousha had known from the time she'd seen the name in the paper. As if the nightmare could not get any worse, the kid allegedly killed by her husband was the nephew of her ex-lover, the street gangster Camp Butterfield. She wondered how long before Camp and his crew came seeking their own justice.

She had ended it over a year ago. She and David had been going through a rough time. He'd been trying to figure out what to do with his life after going from job to job.

Her parents, who had never been crazy about her choice of husband, had been in her business and in her ear way too much. The thing with Camp had been fun for a while, a strong diversion to take her focus off of her own life.

However, she was a mother. Moreover, for better or worse, richer or poorer, in sickness and in health, she was a wife. So she'd broken it off with Camp. To her surprise, he had taken it hard. She'd figured he would easily replace her with one of a myriad of women. It hadn't been that easy, but she didn't have a choice. She was married, but she never shared that part of her life with Camp Butterfield the gangster.

Eventually, things got better between David and her. David got hired by the police department, and it seemed to give him direction and focus. Daria was getting older, and they committed themselves to her. After a few months, the phone calls and texts from Camp had slowed and then stopped.

The lawyer was packing to leave. McGill offered to return the dishes to the kitchen and tidy up. She and David continued to sit mutely on the sofa in stunned silence, each of them in their own thoughts.

"Anousha, what should I do? Maybe we could get the plea deal down further if I say I'm interested?"

"No!" she said quicker and louder than she meant. "It's still very early in this investigation; we still don't know what was going on with that kid."

"Yeah, but I could do serious time for this if it goes the wrong way," David said, scared but reconciled.

"And a lot of police like you are not prosecuted," Anousha said guiltily.

"You mean because I'm white."

"I mean because you are innocent and I love you, and Daria and I need you here."

But David was right. How upside down had the world become when a black woman would be praying for the corrupt, racially one-sided justice system to perform in its typical way.

"Eighteen months is not that long," he said, still looking straight ahead at no one in particular. "Either way, I'm out of the cop business."

Anousha knelt in front of him. She could feel him drifting away from her, accepting what he thought was his fate. David was a man of accountability and fairness, sometimes even to his own detriment. She kissed him and held him close and tight.

"David, we are going to pray and have faith. We are going wait on the Lord to guide us in the way. Please promise me."

"Noush, I don't know if God hears me like he hears you. It's not like I been to church lately."

It was true. David Cooley was Catholic by baptism and part of that group of believers disenchanted by misguided Sunday school teachers and apathetic religious leaders. He was a good-hearted, fair-minded man of integrity, but he didn't know if he believed that all of this was the work of an omnipresent super spirit.

"Baby, God hears everybody who sincerely calls out to him in prayer and need," Anousha pleaded in his ear. "Just promise me that we won't make a decision unless we make it together."

By now, he was holding her close as well. She felt his tears on her neck. They ran silently down her shoulder. He had been crying for some time.

"I just don't want to lose my family and miss Daria's whole life rotting in some jail."

"You won't. We won't let you. He won't let you."

Outside the Cooley's house, McGill stopped to talk to the union lawyer. "How long is that offer on the table,' he asked.

"A few days at least, unless they find more damaging evidence," the lawyer said.

"Copy that. Try to stall them as long as possible; I want my friend to have every chance to clear himself."

"How?"

"I don't know, but he doesn't need the news of a plea offer

getting out. It makes him look guilty and convicted," McGill said earnestly.

"Of course," the lawyer said. "All plea deals are confidential until executed."

"Good. I want to do some legwork on this myself," McGill said, and he turned to walk to his squad car.

## Chapter Nine

The Paladin Crew and I arrived in Atlanta two days later. We used two of the black GMC Yukon SUVs equipped for our cause. Paladin kept four vehicles for this sort of work. It was a considerable expense for an outfit our size, but we made judicious use of them.

Along the way, we picked up two additional operatives. Five other operatives were waiting for us in Atlanta.

TruLuv was a big fan of the Airbnb house rental website. We were stationed in a three-thousand-square-foot Victorian mini-mansion in the Virginia Highlands area.

First order of business, Bobby Sr. and I wanted to check in with the local police department. Most security firms didn't do this, and we got our fair number of odd looks from the police as well. Nevertheless, I thought it was necessary to know who the players were even if we never needed each other. If we did need their services, well, it would be good that we were acquainted.

Bobby Jr and Teri Lovejoy would meet with the other operatives and brief them on their duties. Then they would escort TruLuv to rehearsal.

Uniform officers from all over the city were assigned to the classic, but command belonged to Captain Terry Sayles. He operated out of the main Public Safety Annex near City Hall in the Government District of Atlanta.

Bobby Sr. and I still had a few friends left on the force in St. Louis who felt we'd gotten a raw deal when we'd been dismissed years ago. Some were even in command now. As a favor, they made calls to Atlanta on our behalf.

Captain Sayles was about six feet tall, with medium-brown skin, and in great shape. His uniform fit him like a second skin, showing many hours in the gym. He had a full mustache and a short afro peppered with gray hair. His expression was not hostile but leery. Bobby Sr. and I were used to it.

"So, you two used to wear the badge?" he said. He had a Southern accent but not from Georgia. His eyes constantly flickered at Bobby Sr. in his robotic chair and back to me.

"That's right, Captain. We're on security detail with the TruLuv act. Just wanted to notify your department of our arrival and presence," I explained.

Captain Sayles nodded as if he understood.

"We want to make sure we are in compliance with our actions," I explained. "Paladin is very experienced with events like this, so hopefully, this will be the only time we see each other."

"You got that right," Captain Sayles said. "I got enough going on with this pop-up classic and now the President bringing his circus to town."

"How many officers you got assigned to the fairgrounds?" I asked.

"Not enough," he said. "This Homeland Security cowboy

came in here two days ago, making demands and setting agendas, but did he offer any men or a payment to cover this overtime? Hell no!"

"What about the Secret Service?" Bobby Sr. asked. "Don't you need to coordinate with them?"

"You would think so," Captain Sayles said. "We get all the information we need from the Homeland Security guy, Connors. That president ain't all that popular in certain parts of this town. I don't need him getting shot on my watch. Then I go down in history as being the policeman on the job when the president goes down. No thank you."

Bobby Sr. and I nodded in agreement. It seemed like a conversation that the beleaguered command officer had been having a lot lately.

"What about the mayor and the governor?" I asked.

"I don't know," Captain Sayles said, rubbing his face and checking his watch. "I'm no politician. I'm a cop. I say what I mean and mean what I say. They say they have my back, that we're all on the same team, but . . . what does that mean? You know what I mean, right?"

Bobby Sr. and I nodded.

"Captain, we have some pretty sophisticated equipment we work with. If we can help with anything like drone surveillance, don't hesitate," Bobby Sr. explained.

He was our electronic surveillance expert. Refusing to let a wheelchair slow him down, Bobby Sr. had become the best fifty-something physical specimen he could be above the waist and better at electronic and surveillance equipment than the NSA.

Captain Sayles waved his hand, acknowledging the offer.

"I appreciate you two coming in here like this. A lot of crazy cowboys doing security work are really part security and part hoodlums, carrying loads they don't know how to use."

Bobby Sr. and I made moves to leave.

"Any word on the kid killed near the museum the other night?" I asked. It was a stretch, but I owed it to TruLuv to try. Captain Sayles didn't seem put off by the question.

"Naw, not my detail, but a lot of strong opinions about it. Got protests and counter-protests popping up all over town. Officers on edge. We even had an attempted ambush last night."

"What happened?" I asked.

The captain waved his hand as if he had said too much already, but he kept talking. "Dumbasses over in the Masonville Apartment Complex ran up on an officer sitting in her patrol car. First shot bounced off the metal around the door window. Second shot jammed in their cheap-ass automatic. That was enough time for the officer to bug out."

"They catch who did it?" Bobby Sr. asked.

"Please! I wish," Captain Sayles said, rolling his eyes. "Good day, gentlemen. Be careful out there."

## Chapter Ten

The rear entrance to the ATL Dome was alive with crowds. Word had been leaked on Facebook, Instagram, and the Big Boo Classic website that all the acts would be there. There were thousands in the parking lot, blocking the entrance and accosting every van, limousine, and SUV that arrived.

Local media, podcast broadcasters, and entertainment bloggers were on the scene, which made it the place to be. Selfies and phantom celebrity sightings were rampant. Plus, amateur performers were breaking into song or dance or comedy standup in the parking lot and streaming live. Not everyone was there for the music.

There were protesters with signs that read "No Justice, No Peace" and "Justice for Butta!" They were black and white, old and young, and they were all live streaming. The new face of protest didn't depend on the major press. They were their own press.

And there wouldn't be protesters without counter-protesters. These were all white, with just as many signs and streaming just as hard. Their signs read "Protect the Police" and "Keep Your Hands Off Our Guns!" Between the two groups were Atlanta Metro Police, keeping things orderly.

"Bobby, keep an eye out for the twins somewhere in the crowd. The Ferguson group should be out there somewhere," Teri explained.

"It's a damn circus out there!" Bobby Jr. exclaimed, his head on a swivel as he looked out the windows on both sides of the vehicle.

"Welcome to my world," TruLuv responded. He was in his element. While Teri and Bobby Jr were on heightened alert, TruLuv was smiling and glowing with excitement.

They were in two SUVs. The extra detail was in the first black Yukon. Teri, Bobby Jr., TruLuv, and two additional operatives were in the second. They were in the stop-and-go line of vehicles dropping off talent at the ATL Dome.

"Here's the plan," Teri said to the security crew in the first SUV via digital communicators. "Unit One, secure the entrance. We in Unit Two will secure the package for a brief interaction with the crowd. Then we will move the package inside for rehearsal."

"Unit One copy!" came through the communicator in response.

"TruLuv, brief means brief," Teri said, taking command of the situation. "There are a lot of conflicting interests out there. Let's not make the cops' job any harder."

The rapper raised both hands in agreement.

The Paladin SUVs eventually made their way to the entrance. Unit One jumped out and took their positions. Unit Two escorted TruLuv out onto the porch of the rear entrance. The crowds erupted in cheers, screams, and applause. Even the protesters cheered. TruLuv had a musical message that spoke across racial, gender, and age lines.

Instead of going into the entrance like the other celebrities, TruLuv unexpectedly turned to the crowd, with Teri and Bobby Jr. on either side. As TruLuv addressed the crowd,

Teri scanned the crowd for threats and Chunky and Choppy Wells.

"Hello, Atlanta!" he shouted, and the crowd cheered back. Several brave souls moved forward, trying to get pictures and record videos with their iPads. The security detail attempted to move the crowd back, but TruLuv motioned for them to stand back.

"Keep it brief, kid," Teri said, her head on a swivel. Bobby Jr. was communicating with the security detail.

"I just wanna say that I am out there with you! I am dedicating my performance to the memory of Butta!"

The crowd cheered. Protest signs went up. Counter-protesters were quiet.

"And it won't stop this weekend. I won't stop until we get justice for Butta and a jail sentence for Officer Cooley!"

With that, the crowds went wild in cheers and boos. TruLuv was starting a chant, "No justice, no peace," but Teri and Bobby Jr. moved him forcibly to the rear door of the ATL Dome.

"So much for brief," Bobby Jr. said, looking over at Teri, each of them holding an arm of MC TruLuv, rapper of the common man. They handed him over to two operatives to take him to rehearsal.

"There they are." Bobby Jr. pointed back through the entrance door.

Among the first few rows of protesters, in a jumble of signs and thrust fists, Teri could just make out the repetitive faces of the twins. She was too far away to get their attention, but they'd obviously just seen TruLuv's rally cry. She sent a quick status text to me. Then she and Bobby Jr. headed down the cavernous hall to catch up with TruLuv.

A few twists and turns later down the tunnels under the playing surface of the dome, they caught up with TruLuv and the two operatives. They were talking to another man. He was British, in his twenties, white, and muscular, and he went by the name DJ Supersonic.

"What's up, Double-S?" Bobby Jr. said as they approached. "Didn't know you were coming to this."

"Wouldn't miss it, man. I got to make it to a few shows with this skinny, busy bastard here before he replaces me with Paris Hilton or Brittany Sky," he said jokingly, pointing to TruLuv. The two of them hugged briefly.

Horatio Fuller, aka DJ SuperSonic, had been TruLuv's DJ and musical collaborator from day one. They'd met in high school when they'd been thrown together during study hall. He was six-three, with spiky, dyed-blond hair, freckles, and muscles from head to toe. He was from London originally, coming to the states to get into the music business. He was in his trademark tight black t-shirt and jeans and black brogue boots.

"Ready to rehearse," TruLuv said as he made his way to the stage.

"Just a minute, mate," Supersonic said, holding TruLuv's arm. "There's another act finishing up."

"Oh, that's cool; I'll go say what's up," TruLuv said, even

more excited. He loved visiting with other acts and catching up on where they'd played recently, what venues were like, and good places to eat.

"Hey, Tru, it's Lola, " Supersonic said quickly. "She'll be through in a few minutes."

"Oh," TruLuv said softly. He seemed to actually deflate. "I thought she would have been finished long ago."

Bobby Jr. started to say something encouraging but thought better of it. Teri mentally rolled her eyes. She thought this sounded exactly like something Lola's diva ass would try.

Teri was, like TruLuv, on the fence of forgiveness when it came to Lola Montclaire and her great deception.

The next few minutes were awkward, with Bobby Jr. and Supersonic making small talk about home, new music, and weight-training regimens. When the stage manager came to bring them to the open rehearsal stage, TruLuv was a different person, deflated, quiet, and in no shape to rehearse.

## Chapter Eleven

In the West End/College Town part of the city, two blocks over from Spellman University, there was a bar that serves above-average hamburgers, Reuben's, and beef liver smothered in onions and gravy. It was also a known hangout for cops. The two officers were there having lunch when the server approached the table. She was a small, quiet lady with dark-brown skin, sad eyes, and her hair in a natural bun.

She was holding a note, folded, with both their names on it.

"Who gave you this?" one of them asked.

"Little Japanese dude in the ally out back," the girl said as she bussed the table behind them, removing dishes and swatting crumbs off the chair seats.

They found Kai leaning against a telephone pole, both hands in the pockets of a long leather duster that went past her knees.

"He needs to talk to you," she said, not moving.

A few seconds later, they were in her black Cadillac, the officers in the back seat, she and Camp in the front. As a matter of mutual distrust, they did not use names. Each assumed the other was recording the conversations.

"What the fuck do you two have to do with Cooley?" Camp asked.

"We're officers," one of the officers said. "I—"

"Listen to me; my little cousin just got gunned down by a cop. I pay you two to make sure this does not happen."

"Sorry, I—" the other one started to say, but Camp wasn't having it.

"Where have you two been? I been calling you for three days."

"Out there beating the bushes for you. We didn't know who this Cooley guy was. He seems like a boy scout, but boy scouts don't usually go cowboy like that."

"He says he shot in the air, trying to warn Butta to stop," Kai said.

"Yeah, I don't know if I believe that," one said.

"You say you don't know him?" Camp said more than asked.

Both officers nodded.

"So, what did you find out in the last three days? What's up with this mufucka, man?" Camp asked. "Is he the boy scout everybody sayin' he is? Because, if he is, then this shit don't make no sense."

"Cops don't patrol by themselves. The news doesn't say who the other cops were on the scene?" Kai asked.

"Not sure," one said.

"Well, you can find the fuck out," Camp said.

"We definitely can find out; we are here to get you whatever you need," the other officer said.

"Can you kill David Cooley for us?" Kai asked flatly.

The car was quiet for several seconds. Then she laughed softly.

"She just fuckin' with you'll," Camp said. "But whatever information you can get me, the better. This just doesn't feel like an accident."

"Maybe Cooley's on somebody's payroll," one officer said. "Butta was up near Disciple Daniels's territory."

"You tell me!" Camp said. "Find out and don't be all week."

More nods from the officers.

"Get the fuck outta here and earn your cheese," Kai said.

The cops quickly got out of the car. Camp and Kai watched them as they walked back into the restaurant.

"What's our next move?" Kai asked.

"Same," Camp said. "We still taking Cooley out. Not waiting on the court system to loophole him out of it."

"What about Anousha?" Kai asked. "And their baby?"

"They'll live. Me and her was dead a long time ago. I just want Cooley."

## Chapter Twelve

That evening, I set up a meeting with my security team, TruLuv, and Chunky and Choppy Wells.

"Tell me how your day went," I asked the twins. "What did you see today?"

"Just a bunch of yelling and sign holding," Choppy said. His voice was hoarse. "A lot of people down here are just here to be on the scene. Taking selfies and uploading to Instagram. Amateur rappers, singers, and people selling bootleg purses. But there are some serious ones on both sides."

"How so?" Teri asked.

"We actually had dinner with counter-protesters," Choppy said with a sly smile.

"What? Where?" I asked, not believing my hearing.

"Not a smart thing to do," Teri said.

"It was cool," Choppy explained. "As the protest slowed down, people started to disperse. A group of us went to McDonald's for lunch. When we got there, we saw a group of counter-protesters already there eating."

"Sounds like a good day to have Burger King," I said.

"Couldn't do that, Lem; go somewhere else because of some cracka'-ass protesters?" Choppy said.

"So, how does this not turn into a police event?" I asked.

"We were all eating, them at their table and us at ours. That particular McDonalds plays music. In the middle of lunch, Drake comes on the radio, followed by DJ Khalid, followed by Cardi B."

"And?" I said.

"And before you know it, we are all singing. We started off trying to out-sing each other, but then we were all singing along and high-fiving," Choppy explained.

Bobby Sr. and I looked at each other. I could not believe what I was hearing.

"Did you all exchange a bottle of Coke and a smile?" I asked.

The twins just looked as if they didn't understand. I waved the comment off.

"It wasn't all of them or all of us," Choppy explained. "But a few of us had a serious conversation. It started off with names and cities we were from. We talked about football, music, television. A few of us talked about video games."

"And you never talked about the protests?" I asked.

"Oh, yeah," Choppy said. "We knew where the other one stood. It didn't take much talk. Their biggest concern was safety."

"Safety?"

"So, there was this kid name Hunter. He was here with his sister. They wanted to have their say and support law enforcement. Their dad and granddad were cops. But they got down here and got swept up in this Confederate, whites-first wave of protest. He just wants to get back to Albany, Georgia, in one piece."

"Why doesn't he just go home now?" Bobby Sr. asked.

"Because that would be like being run off by the assholes. The same reason they wanted to demonstrate for law enforcement is the same reason to stay and not let the rednecks' message be the only message."

"But why is their safety in question?" I asked single-mindedly.

"Some of these demonstrators are just thugs looking for a fight. They can't even discuss the issues. It's just, 'Let's smash this; let's burn that,'" Choppy explained.

"Did Hunter or his sister give any names? Point any of them out?" Teri asked.

The twins shook their heads.

"But it's crazy on both sides," Chunky Wells said. "There's a group calling themselves the New Revolutionaries, some brothas out of Wichita, Kansas. They are actually talking about putting a bounty out on Cooley."

"What kind of bounty?" I asked.

"Cash," Chunky said. "We heard twenty thousand first; then fifty thousand."

"Have you met any of these New Revolutionaries?" I asked.

The twins shook their heads.

We talked out tomorrow's schedule. Then I had two

operatives drive the twins back to their hotel. We reminded them and the rest of the Ferguson group to be careful.

## Chapter Thirteen

Thursday morning was the start of the classic weekend. The Big Boo Classic promotion machine was in full swing. Morning television news was full of human interest stories about everything from the musical acts to the concession workers.

There was a full-page newspaper ad showing the schedule of events from Thursday to Sunday. Facebook ads invited members to download the Big Boo App, which showed every event hour by hour.

There was regular news as well. Two articles, in particular, would end up having a bigger effect on the day's events than anything else.

Just below the front-page fold of the *Atlanta Times* was the headline: "How Well Do We Know Shawn Butterfield?"

The article focused on the dead drum major's upbringing in the rough-and-tumble-turned-gentrified East Atlanta neighborhood. It devoted four paragraphs to his criminal past: arrests for theft, drug possession, and disturbing the peace. There were only two paragraphs, though, on his resurgence as a successful college student and musician. The writer had made a few cynical remarks about Butta's vegetarian reputation and the fact that he was killed with a meat sandwich in his hand.

The second article was an op-ed piece about Camp Butterfield. The writer questioned whether Shawn had been working for his cousin and been killed on his way to do something criminal. He inferred that maybe Shawn, who dressed like Camp most of the time, had been mistaken for his "kingpin cousin."

While factually accurate, both were far from impartial. Both writers were obviously pro-law enforcement.

I wondered if pieces like this were created more for the conservative readers or to promote the ire of black folks and liberals who read and re-read the piece and inevitably boosted "clicks, views, and reacts," the old adage being: "Any press is good press."

My first call was to the operatives. Despite my protestations that I couldn't do it, I did put people in the protest crowds to watch Chunky and Choppy Wells. I was not as warm and cozy as they were after hearing about their kumbaya experience in the McDonalds. Maybe it was because I was a sixties baby, but it felt unnatural to me.

My next call was to Captain Sayles. After some backdoor creeping on the dark web, Bobby Sr. and I had found the sites for the New Revolutionaries. We'd sent the links to the police last night.

"I turned it over to our cybercrime unit. So far, there's a lot of bluster and talk," Captain Sayles explained. "We'll continue to monitor them without them seeing us. I wanna see if anyone takes them up on their offer. Then we will catch them all."

"We think we got a line on some white supremacist groups amongst the counter-protesters," Bobby Sr. said.

"You guys aren't out there doing police work, are you?" Captain Sayles said with admonishment in his tone.

"No, no," I said. "We hear and see things on both sides of the protest. People talk around security, not realizing we still have eyes and ears."

Captain Sayles thanked us for the intel. "I didn't realize you had a connection to the dead drum major."

"Uh, ummm ?" I said.

"Your client, Tru-Luv," Captain Sayles said flatly, as if he were reading it. "He was some kind of mentor to the dead kid?"

"Right," I said.

"See, we do our homework too, Lemon Boy!" he said with a laugh. "I thought I would do some checking after you asked yesterday."

"Oh," I said a little sheepishly.

"Your nickname? I get it. It's because you're light-skinned."

"Right, but people call me Lem. And yes, Shawn's death hit close to home for TruLuv."

 "I get it," he replied, turning serious again. "It's a fucked-up business. Don't see how Cooley escapes jail time on this. They have been trying to confirm the ricochet, scouring the trees in the area. So far, nothing."

"What about the ballistics and forensics?" I asked, figuring all he could say was no.

"Haven't seen it yet, but on something like this, I'm not surprised it's taking longer."

We said goodbye. Then he added, "Lem, I owe you for this intel. I can't tell you everything, but I will share what I can about the Butterfield-Cooley case as it comes across."

"Thanks, Captain," Bobby Sr. said. "We'll get you that info on the skinheads soon."

\*\*\*

Later that morning, we accompanied TruLuv to the International Plaza Fairgrounds, adjacent to the ATL Dome. In the main tent was the Youth Symposium and Health Fair.

"Teri, take your detail and get posted at the health screening booth," I said. "We'll be over once TruLuv finishes his time with the kids."

"Copy that," she replied and motioned for her two operatives to follow her. As I watched them go, they appeared odd. She was five three, and the operatives were well over six feet. All three were wearing the same black cargo pants, black polo, and boots. Little did anyone know that it was Teri, the petite female, who had the skills to kill you with her bare hands.

"Any word from Bobby Jr.?" I asked his father, who was next to me.

"Not yet, but it's early," Bobby Sr. said. "He needs time to melt into the scene."

The night before, we set a plan to insert Bobby Jr. undercover amongst the counter-protesters with the plan that he identify with and get close to the white supremacists. If we had something to worry about, I wanted to know about it as soon as possible.

We'd set him up with dual cameras, one in a skull pendant on a cord necklace and the other in his Confederate flag belt buckle. This was some of our newest equipment, borrowed from some military friends we'd met in North Carolina. The camera feeds uploaded directly to the cloud. That way, if the cameras were damaged or compromised in the field, the intel was not lost.

TruLuv, in the meantime, was in his element. Moving among the elementary and junior high school kids, he was as comfortable as a child himself. They begged him to dance and rap, but he refused until he saw what they could do. How did he know there would be at least ten children with routines ready to show him?

Before we knew it, he had a mini-concert going that drew kids and adults from all around the tent to watch. He became totally oblivious to his celebrity as he joined in song with one student and mimicked the dance steps of others. I got a glimpse of the kid he had been ten years ago, a glimpse of the kid that I had missed.

## Chapter Fourteen

Gina Pombo was busy at that moment rehearsing for Battle of the Bands and Saturday's halftime show in the gym at Birmingham A&M. She was full of excitement. And dread.

She'd always known that one day, she would get her chance to perform with the Marching Pride at halftime on the fifty-yard line. She'd worked day and night, weekends and holidays, to be perfect in her routines. Any mistakes, any missed steps, any wrong turns would give some of her male counterparts the ammunition they wanted to kick her out of the drum corps. They would like nothing more than to send her back to the flutes.

Now she was getting her chance, and she never felt so scared or alone.

When she'd first raised her hand to try out for drum major, Butta had been the only man in the entire band who hadn't laughed. She'd even lost some of her female friends, either out of jealousy or so that they could court favor with a particular male member of the band.

Then there were the rumors and sniggling of her being gay, which she thought was the dumbest thing to whisper about in 2017 even if it had been true.

Her father, Henry Pombo, spent his life behind the wheel as a bus and limousine driver in Dallas, Texas. He'd seen a lot and always dreamed and talked of bigger and better things. He was an avid reader of Zig Ziglar, Tony Robbins, and Les Brown. He'd sent Gina off to Birmingham A&M with a band scholarship, eighteen hundred dollars cash, and a head full of ambitions and dreams. She could not stand the idea of disappointing her father. She had not even told him about the Classic and her promotion to one of the lead drum majors just in case it didn't actually happen.

*Butta would know exactly what to say to me*, she thought. *He always knew.*

His smile and his encouragement were as regular as the sunrise, and she didn't realize how much she missed him until now. When she'd been having trouble working the scepter, Butta had worked with her in the city parks before class and on weekends after football season. They'd talked of running the drum corps together when they were seniors, alternating as lead drum major. They'd even gotten in shape together. She'd admired his exercise record. Rain or shine, even if Butta hadn't gone to class, he'd still worked out.

She'd always wondered why he'd never made a pass at her. They'd had fun together, but it had been more like they were cousins. He hadn't even done the not-so-innocent flirting all guys did, but he'd been a good friend. Now he was gone, just like that, and she felt like she were trying to dance with one shoe.

"To hell with that," she said to no one particular. "I won't let Butta down."

"You talking to yourself?" a male voice asked behind her. "Or you praying?"

It was Milton Clark, a senior and the most senior of the drum corps. Milton was everything a drum major should be: tall, fit, proud, and a showman. Even now, he was standing in the doorway like a movie actor from a bygone age or a well-dressed member of some Motown act. He had dark skin that seemed to glow as if he wore makeup. His hair was some curly textured style that always looked fresh out of the shop. However, Gina noticed that he always had cold eyes that never smiled. He was smiling now, but it was the grin of a barracuda.

"Hey, MC," she said, silently cursing the weakness of her voice. "Just getting myself tight for Saturday."

"Yeah, well, that's if you get on the field at all," he said, walking towards her. "I mean, we can just go with two drum majors."

He was correct. Initially, that had been the discussion. The Marching Pride always took the field with their signature three drum majors. With Butta's death, they'd thought about going with Milton and Jesse Isaacs, the third lead drum major.

The problem was that the routine didn't work with two drum majors, and there was not enough time to redo the routine.

Next on the list to take Butta's spot were Gina and a freshman named Allen Carter. Allen had broken his foot pledging a fraternity.

Then rumors had surfaced about emergency tryouts. Inquiries had been made to former drum majors who had graduated. Then there'd been talk of borrowing drum majors from other schools. For major network television, the Marching Pride had to have their signature three drum majors – the Roaring III.

That was when she'd gone to the music department, not demanding, but boldly asking for her rightful spot on the field. Madina Sherman had been on campus that day, and through divine intervention, she'd heard about Gina as Butta's replacement. Madina had loved the idea, and in a matter of one day, Gina had gone from persona non grata to the reason Battle of the Bands programs had to be reprinted.

Milton walked up to her until he was close. He smelled like sandalwood and hair oil.

"What's up, man," Gina asked.

For several seconds, he stood perfectly still, looking down on her with those dead eyes. Then he exhaled and said, "I stand next to you, Pombo, and instantly, my nose is filled with the smell of fear and vagina juice."

She just took a step back, looking at him incredulously.

"I mean, what are you trying to get done here? All of you bitches trying to be drum majors? What is that about? You not fine enough for Pride Dancers, so you coming up here to lead the field."

"MC, I was always a drum major, even in high school," Gina said, feeling around inside for her courage. "Don't worry. I'll hold my own."

"Do I look worried, GEE-NA?" he said, sounding like Martin Lawrence on the iconic sitcom. "I have been a part of this line for five years. I got Battle of the Bands trophies for the last three years. This classic will be on ESPN, not ESPNU. I won't have any slips."

"I won't slip," Gina said defiantly.

"Oh, really," Milton replied, moving in on her. "When the lights come on and the network cameras are rolling and the crowd is cheering so loud you can't hear yourself think?"

He pushed his body against hers.

"When the camera phones are live streaming," he continued, his voice taking on a husky whisper. "You not gonna choke on your own spit, lose your step, get off rhythm from Jesse and me . . ."

He pushed her the rest of the way against the mirrored wall.

"And sweat from every stank-ass pore."

He reached down and roughly swiped his long brown hand between her legs and against her center. Then he held it up to his nose and made a face.

Gina's silence was more from astonishment than fear. She was used to the bravado of band members and especially drum majors. This had turned into some other dirty, ugly thing that had come on her before she'd realized it.

Her head and ears were full of the sound of her breath and the beat of her heart. When she found her voice, she pushed off the wall and kicked up for his testicular region. He slid rather than jumped backward with Gregory Hines smoothness.

Gina was in a full defensive crouch. He laughed a low

chuckle and continued to step back with light steps, his dead eyes never leaving her face. She watched him slowly stroll out of the gym.

## Chapter Fifteen

**Main Event Tent – International Plaza Fairgrounds**

Teri and her operatives were watching the health fair. TruLuv, who was entertaining children on the other side, was supposed to have worked the entire tent by now, but it seemed like he was stuck with the kids.

She was listening to a young lady, Brianna Daniels, who'd been crowned Miss Birmingham A&M during Homecoming four weeks ago. Today, young Brianna was in Homecoming garb: sparkling blue gown, gold title sash, but no crown. Bria was medium brown and small framed. She was about five foot five, with shoulder-length black hair with reddish-blonde highlights. She spoke with conversational hand gestures, and her eyes widened with each point. She looked regal and mature on stage, but her laugh during jokes harkened back to childhood.

She was talking to a group of junior high schoolers about self-esteem, appearance, respect, completing high school, and setting goals.

She was articulate and funny. There were some nerves, but Teri figured it was just an uncomfortableness with public speaking. That was what twenty-year-olds looked like.

Then she finished her speech and waved goodbye to the students. About ten seconds later, Teri heard a thump like a body hitting the floor. She turned back to the stage and could just make out the bottom of the blue gown behind the curtain separating the stage from backstage.

Teri was on the run. Barking commands into her communicator mic clipped to her shoulder loop, she pushed past the volunteers standing around the downed homecoming queen.

"Call 911! And find a first aid kit," she barked, and people went running. She turned Bria onto her back. She found a pulse and saw Bria was breathing. In a few seconds, Teri had the rear zipper to her dress lowered and open enough to make sure she was not injured.

Bria came to just before the ambulance arrived.

"My name is Teri," she said holding her face close to the collapsed coed. "Do you know where you are?"

"O-On the floor," Bria responded groggily and with a little fear in her voice.

"On the floor where?"

Bria responded correctly. Then paramedics were on the scene.

"She's female, early twenties, appears to be suffering from a syncopal episode," Teri explained. "Pulse and breathing are normal. Eye dilation is sluggish but reasonably responsive."

The paramedics gave the small security woman with obvious medical knowledge a brief quizzical look before jumping into action on the patient, who was trying to rise to a sitting position.

Teri eased into the background and let them do their work. The paramedics went through the protocol, asking Brianna for:

Her name?

Address?

Purpose for being where she was?

How had she arrived?

Over the next few minutes, she responded with better mental acuity as medical personnel repeated the routine questions and her vitals were checked.

Brianna continued to refuse medical attention and a ride to the hospital. However, a volunteer spoke up.

"Sweetie, I'm afraid you don't have a choice. Medical emergencies at classic sanctioned events that result in ambulance response must include, but not be limited to, examination by physicians immediately after the event."

She was a light-brown woman in her sixties. She had small freckles across her nose and cheeks and tight ringlet curls in her light-brown and gray hair, and she seemed to be the leader of the other volunteers. Her nametag read "Gayle."

Brianna relented, maybe more from fatigue than the dictates of the prim, direct official volunteer. Teri followed the gurney out of the large event tent and onto the emergency response vehicle. The lead volunteer was standing there as well

"What do you think?" Teri asked her.

Gayle continued to look at the departing ambulance, her dire expression never changing. "Hmmmm-mm," was her only response to Teri's question.

***

That afternoon, Bobby Sr., Teri, TruLuv, and I met back at the house. The seven operatives were split, four at the house and the other three in the field.

While they were comparing notes over an Italian dinner carryout from La Tavola, I was on the phone with my mother.

"So, those twins behaving themselves?" Mama asked. "I know that Choppy can be a handful."

"So far, so good," I explained. My mother had seen the video streams of the twins' battle singing with white kids in a local McDonalds. I chose not to mention the operatives I had in the field keeping an eye on them. It would just make her worry even more.

"How are you and TruLuv coming with the work on the case?" she asked.

"There is no case, Mama."

"TruLuv has some things he wanted to get done while he was there. So that cop doesn't get off. So that justice is done."

"I know, but he's not a police officer or a detective."

"Yes, but you are there," she said in a tone that said, "Duh!"

"Look, he shared his information and his theories with me, but I don't know that it will help. It could hinder things."

"Well, I see they are doing everything to sully the dead,"

Mama said. "I read that awful story about poor Shawn. Show me a kid, black or white, who hasn't made a mistake or two. How would they like their kids' transgressions printed all over the newspaper?"

"I know."

"And none of the coverage of his accomplishments, six straight semesters on the dean's list, scheduled to graduate in three years, Governor's Council for Fitness, and active church member."

"Mmm-hmmm.".

"And what about this thug cousin of his, this Camp the story alluded to? Why hasn't he come forward and told the public that his cousin was innocent?"

"I don't know; no one has heard from him."

"MMMM-mmmm," she said.

The phone was silent for several seconds. I took a sip of my Booker's on the rocks and readied to get off the phone.

"Soooo, how about your other job? How is Lola? Has TruLuv talked to his mother?"

"No," I said.

"NO!"

"I mean not yet; Mama, we just got here," I said plaintively, sensing what was coming. I took another deep drag on my Booker's.

"Well, Darryl, what have you done? You have not helped

TruLuv in his work to make sure that dead boy gets justice. You haven't worked on mending your family."

"There is Chunky and Choppy," I mumbled.

"Well, thank God for that," she said. These admonishments were not as harsh as they sounded. Verna Phillips prided herself that any young person she worked with were going to be better as a result of it.

This verbal browbeating was one of her ways of bringing that out. The fact that I was a grown ass man didn't excuse me from the treatment. I was still 'young people' to her.

"Don't just sit there on the phone clinking that liquor ice in my ear. What are your plans? And don't tell me you ain't got one."

"Plan for what?" I mumbled trying to pull my thoughts together.

"For anything," she said her tone sharp as a corner on a cheap countertop.

"TruLuv has a series of interviews. During those, he's going to tell the better side of Shawn. I made some inquiries about the ballistics report. I'm pretty sure I can get a copy. I fig. . . "

"Ok, that was what I wanted to hear," Mama said with finality. "Now get that boy and his mama together and you would have earned your keep."

"Thanks, Mama," I said shaking my head but smiling.

"You welcome. Now don't drink too much; you got a long day tomorrow."

"OK, Mama. Love you."

"I loved you first," she said. Then she hung up the phone before getting too sentimental.

Sitting at the large kitchen island with the granite top, I passed her love to TruLuv, who actually blushed. Dinner consisted of tomato basil spaghetti and tagliatelle Bolognese, bread, and grilled asparagus.

For a skinny kid, TruLuv actually ate a lot. I had been around a lot of musical, stage, and cinematic talent. All of them either smoked, drank, talked, or slept to excess. Not one of them ate enough to fill a hummingbird. That was not the case with TruLuv. He ate and didn't seem to gain an ounce, a trait from Lola's side of the family.

Teri was sitting next to me on my left. TruLuv was to my right, and Bobby Sr. was across from me, on the opposite side of the kitchen island.

"You got your notes ready for your interviews with the entertainment media?" I asked TruLuv.

"Oh yeah, but I will steer the conversations to Shawn and his murder. They will get to know the real Butta, the kid I met last year."

"You got to know him pretty good, huh?" Bobby Sr. asked.

"I think so; he was still raw in his talent, but after learning of his journey, I realized he had come a long way in an amazingly short amount of time."

TruLuv repeated Butta's story of a life that had pivoted from street thug to musical prodigy.

"You ever meet his cousin, this Camp Butterfield?" Bobby Sr. asked.

"No. Shawn spoke of him a lot; it was obvious that they loved each other like brothers. Shawn still dressed like him, even copied his walk, from what I hear."

"And we're sure it wasn't a case of mistaken identity?" Bobby Sr. asked.

"Not likely," TruLuv said. "I understand Camp Butterfield has some weight in the streets. He's not likely to have been running on foot through Centennial Park."

"That's only part of my concern," I said. "We still don't know where Butta was going that night."

"Yeah, I already spoke with his mother," TruLuv said. "She admitted to me that she didn't know he was in town."

"What did she tell the police?" I asked.

"Nothing, she never answered the question about where he was headed."

"That could make him look guilty," Bobby Sr. said.

"Looking guilty and being guilty are still two different things," TruLuv snapped back.

Bobby Sr. held up his hands in capitulation.

"Next, where are his cousin and his crew?" I asked rhetorically. "I've known a lot of street criminals; Butta's death screams for revenge."

"We've done some asking around in the right circles," Bobby

Sr. said.

TruLuv looked dubiously at my hardboiled partner.

"Sometimes, white officers will talk to me about alleged black felons quicker than they will talk to Lem," Bobby Sr. said unapologetically.

TruLuv looked back at me; I smiled and shrugged.

"The police are speculating about his cousin. Some say he is biding his time to make his move. Others are saying Shawn's murder was a hit by a rival gang. So, right now, he doesn't know who to hit."

"We can't have him doing anything stupid; that would just hurt our case against Cooley," TruLuv deduced. "We need to reach out to him."

"No, we don't," I said. "If he is in attack mode, it would not be a good look for you to reach out to him at all."

"I'm not worried about my image, Lem!"

"I'm talking about your life, man," I said louder than I intended, and I lowered my voice. "If this guy is as bad as the talk going around, the least that can happen is that your brand takes a hit."

"Maybe Shawn's mother can tell me how to reach him?"

"Did you not hear what I just said, Tru?" I said as loud as I intended that time.

"Of course, but I simply don't agree," he answered.

Beneath the island table, Teri silently pushed the edge of her boot heel into the side of my leg. It was enough to help me gain my composure and not explode on my intelligent, talented, yet naïve son.

"Ok, I respect that," I said calmly while trying to stay the agitation that I was sure was showing on my face. "Consider this, if you will. A person like Camp Butterfield lives a life of mistrust. Anyone approaching him is there to take, not to help. No one ever comes to him for his benefit."

"So?" TruLuv said. "What would someone like me want to take from him? He knows that I was Shawn's mentor."

"Does he? We don't know that for sure. And the question is the same. What do you really want? Maybe you're working for the police? You're a rapper, so maybe you got arrested for some dumb charge. To clean your record, you offer to help the police with this."

Teri picked up the thought process. "Maybe you blame Camp for Butta's death. You feel that it's somehow connected to his business, and you want him brought to justice for the kid's death."

TruLuv was giving these scenarios some thought.

"Maybe you do have good intentions, but you unwittingly bring trouble to his door because the cops have been following everyone closely related to the case, including you."

TruLuv was silent.

"Lem and Teri are saying we have to examine every angle before we make a wrong turn and, instead of helping the story, become the story," Bobby Sr. explained in a subtler voice than I could muster at the time.

TruLuv nodded, and I exhaled.

"Anything else," Teri asked, urging me to continue.

"Oh yeah. I was wondering, what was the reason for the change? What happened two years ago that brought about Butta's transformation?"

"Funny, I never asked him," TruLuv said, showing some embarrassment at not knowing. "When we met, he was well on his way. I saw no semblance of the thug he claimed to have been. We talked about music, performance, and the band."

"You never talked about women?" I asked.

"Of course, but not about anyone in particular," TruLuv said.

"You got the idea he liked girls?" Bobby Sr. asked.

"Oh yeah," TruLuv said, giving it more thought. "That summer we worked together on campus, he was quite popular and did his share of flirting. I got the idea he was trying to stay uncommitted because he knew his music was taking him places."

"What kind of places?" I asked.

"Oh, you know, traveling with the music. He asked a lot about when I started. How did I get on my first tour? where did I go? Did my Au . . . did Lola help me? He seemed more turned on by that than just chasing females."

"Very mature for someone that age," Teri said reflectively.

"He was that guy," TruLuv said

## Chapter Sixteen

Three hours later, we were gearing up to head out to the Big Boo Step Show at the Kopleff Recital Hall on the campus of Georgia State. TruLuv was part of a panel of celebrity judges. Two of the four operatives would head into the field to relieve the other three placed there earlier. The last two would come with us to the step show.

There was a large room at the rear of our rental house. It was about forty feet by twenty, with light wood floors and windows facing the back of the property. In its mid-nineteenth-century heyday, this room must have held private balls where everyone had worn formal clothing, danced in a line under crystal glass chandeliers, and drunk punch served by properly toned negroes in black tails and with lowered eyes.

Tonight, the room housed our operation. Our weapons cache was stored in a steel locker in one corner. The long walls were perfect for posting our timeline. Despite a lot of technology, we were an old-school operation. We set up a series of white grease boards and tacked them to the walls. We set up a schedule of who was working where and when. There was an electronic copy as well. That was in the opposite corner from the weapons.

Bobby Sr.'s command center looked like something out of the headquarters of the CIA. During our first assignments, it had been one man on one laptop. Now it was six screen monitors attached to several laptops through docking stations. There was a Wi-Fi tower that was satellite synced and solar powered. It provided a signal wherever we worked.

Three of the monitors showed the location of operatives in the field. A fourth screen showed the approximate location of Chunky and Choppy Wells.

As a surprise, we had given the Ferguson Force for Change upgraded VIP badges that would get them into all events during the classic. Choppy had said it was a waste of money, as they were there to protest. Chunky had reminded him that they could have some time off. There were no protests during the night events.

The twins' badges were chipped with location transponders and heat sensors. If the badges were removed from their bodies at any time during the day, the chips would register the heat reduction. Right now, the twins were in the vestibule of the Kopleff Concert Hall, at the Big Boo Step Show. From their movement patterns, they were probably in line for concessions.

The last two monitors were devoted to active work. From here, Bobby Sr. handled scheduling, adjustments, assignments, ongoing Paladin business, and what he called his pet projects.

To call him our electronics expert was an understatement. Aside from bench pressing more than me and his son, Bobby Jr., he'd emerged as a bit of a computer and electronics whiz. He handled our encryption and decryption, he managed our electronic surveillance, and lately, he had been dabbling in monitoring the notorious side of social media known as the dark web.

Tonight, he had the GPS map of where Shawn Butta

Butterfield had been killed. On the next and last screen were shots from the SweetSpot video. Teri was getting strapped into her vest and other equipment. Bobby Sr. had been working on the concept of the bullet ricochet. He hadn't had much success due to the poor quality and lighting of the video.

She thought about my question from earlier, the idea of where Butta was going that night. He certainly hadn't been dressed for the club, so the SweetSpot was out. She looked at the bundle of apartments and condos further north.

Looking at the screen, she felt the possibilities were endless. Her eyes glazed over as she examined the grid of neighborhoods, focusing on nothing distinct. At first. Her eyes glanced over it and kept moving before her brain made the connection. Did she see what she thought she saw? She had to retrace her eye path back over the map. She found it. About four streets north and three streets to the east on the GPS grid of where Butta was shot.

Seeing it in writing triggered the auditory memory of it.

"I need to catch up with you later," she said to us as we were getting ready to leave.

"Something wrong?" I asked.

"No, something may be very right, but I got to check it out first; I gotta do it tonight before the trail gets cold," she explained.

"Fine, but you need an operative to go with you," I said, not sure what she was going on about, but I knew from her look that I wasn't going to get much out of her now. Teri hated being wrong. If she wasn't sure about something, she didn't even want to verbalize her hunch. Her hunches, however, were seldom wrong.

"Darryl, I . . ." she started to say, but she could tell from my face I wasn't debating it.

If she wanted to be cryptic, fine, but she would have backup. She agreed to the tag-along operative.

"You got two hours, little sis," I said, strapping up. "Then I'm pulling your string."

## Chapter Seventeen

David Cooley was sitting in the pews at Grace and Mercy Catholic Church off Glenwood Drive. He had not stepped inside a house of worship since the eighth grade.

It wasn't religious conviction that had driven him there this time.

He had been stuck in the house for days. He couldn't watch anymore Netflix.

Watching TV or the internet eventually put him face to face with his news story. Computerized algorithmic artificial intelligence built into the internet figured anyone surfing the web in the Greater Atlanta area wanted to see the hottest news story in town.

The union lawyer, McGill, and now Brody had been back to the house multiple times. They were discussing another plea deal for jail time. McGill, who had been against it, was now changing his tune. David was being tried in the court of public opinion, and it was hard to tell who was winning.

The National Fraternal Order of Police had made statements endorsing a fair hearing. However, the local chapter of the NAACP had revoked an award they had bestowed on him two years prior for his volunteer work in the black community. The AFL-CIO was calling for an internal investigation of the entire police department.

National media compared his story to other stories of outright police brutality – Eric Garner, Michael Brown, and

Walter Scott. Civic organizations he had worked with and felt kinship with were vilifying him openly and publicly.

He felt the walls closing in on him. He was making Anousha crazy with his alternating rants and sobs. Whenever the real horror of accidentally killing the kid and going to prison for life descended upon his psyche, it filled him with terror. She didn't say it, but he could see disappointment and disgust in Anousha's face every time they made eye contact.

Just after dinner, she took Daria to her room to read stories. Later, he found them fast asleep. The house's new solitude, absent of even the non-verbal resonances of human activity, just made the walls close in more.

When he couldn't stand it any longer, he wrote a note for Anousha and deftly walked out the backyard to his personal vehicle parked in a garage just off the alley.

Once on the road, he realized his new problem. Where could he go and not be recognized? Even the thought of continuing to drive around felt like raw danger.

He kept imagining being seen at a traffic stop or being recognized while going down I-75 and all hell breaking loose. He turned left off Moreland Avenue SE and avoided other major streets. He drove around some neighborhoods, sitting low in his seat, wishing he had a ball cap, especially when the lights of oncoming traffic illuminated his face. After a few reactive turns, he came to Grace and Mercy Catholic Church. He suddenly remembered churches in cowboy and science fiction movies being a kind of sanctuary for all who entered.

"How long we going to do this," Kai asked Camp. "We been sitting in this car and watching the house for two damn days."

The two were in one of Kai's vehicles, which were all some form of Cadillac. Today, it was a dark-silver XT5. One thing was becoming clear to her. This task of killing David Cooley was wearing on the boss. Every day, he was less the calm-thinking gangster, single-minded in his pursuit. He was rambling and nervous. He was a mess: his clothes were crinkled, his hair was uncombed, and razor stubble was all over his face.

Plus, there was no plan. Kai had staked out the Cooley house practically around the clock. She'd moved around to several vantage points near the house but not too close. They'd alternated shifts between Kai, Camp, and a contract hired gun named Mohead just in case Cooley traveled while Camp and Kai were otherwise detained. Every day, Camp would appear in what seemed to be some of the same clothes from the day before.

Cadillac Kai Davis had killed at least seven people, going back to her mother's boyfriend, who had put his hands on her mother and her. She'd never been caught because she was patient, she did not talk, and she always had a plan. It wasn't until this week that it had dawned on her that she had never seen or heard about Camp killing anyone. He had a reputation for being ruthless, for rolling with a gang of killers, and even for having it done by people like MoHead, but never him personally.

"For as long as it takes, CK," he answered in that same preoccupied whisper. His breath smelled like cigarettes, alcohol, and stale meat. "Cooley's got to come out of that house sometime."

"But we still got to deal with that sentry watching the house," Kai said. There had been a squad car and patrolman parked in front of the Cooley house almost non-stop since the shooting.

"I see that," Camp answered. "There may be collateral damage."

That sounded like crazy talk to her. They were talking about killing a cop, but they had a reason, a moral imperative. To Kai, that made a difference. Killing someone because they were just in the way was something else.

"When we do this?" she asked. "What's our plan for the heat that will come our way."

"We didn't do it, and they can't prove it."

"And . . . "

"And that's it," he said, taking his eyes off the house and looking at her for the first time.

"Camp, the minute Cooley is put away, we will have every cop in the state looking at us. Did you see the paper this morning?"

She held up a copy of the *Times*, page two, above the fold.

"Camp Butterfield? Should the police be worried?"

It was a story detailing the relationship between Camp and his deceased cousin. It detailed the crimes Camp and his gang were tied to but for which they had never been charged. It detailed how Camp was tied to Central American drug networks doing business underground all across the country.

"That shit's old news," Camp said, thumping the paper.

"Yeah, well, our connects south of the border won't like the attention," Kai reminded him.

"I got a dead cousin and an aunt that wishes she could die," he said. "Now, let's say I do nothing. Huh? Just sit back and play this smart, the long game, like you say."

"Right," Kai said.

"What does that look like to our friends from Medellin and Belize City? Better yet, what does it look like to them greedy niggas up around Cobb County and that slick-ass gambling preacher backed by the Russians? We look weak; we look like we ripe for picking. Then we gotta drop a lot of bodies. This way? We got just one, maybe two."

Kai hated to admit it, but Camp was making perfect gangster sense. Every other set in Atlanta was rife with gunplay, death, destruction, police confiscation, and turnover at the top. These gangs had waited too long to address internal problems, to do the smart thing. Plus, they paid their people poorly, so their profits were constantly being skimmed off of.

Camp's operation didn't have some dumb-ass name spray-painted all over town. He and Kai didn't hang out with entertainers or internet celebrities. His operations had run long and strong for almost seven years because they paid their people well and cut out garbage soldiers at the first sign of laziness or disloyalty.

She didn't like this plan, but she understood this was a defining moment for them. All their enemies in the Atlanta underworld were watching.

Just then, they saw a tan Hyundai come out of the alley behind the Cooley's house at the end of the block.

"Oh shit, it's him," Kai said. "I know the make and model!"

"Are you sure?" Camp asked. "It might be Anousha and the baby."

They watched as the car turned away from them, onto to the side street. Halfway through the turn, the evening light was just right. They could see that it was Cooley and that he was alone. They looked back to the front of the house. The patrol hadn't moved.

"He's sneaking out from under the watch?" Camp said. "Where the hell is he going?"

"What do you wanna do?" Kai asked, starting the engine.

Camp thought for a few seconds. "Let me out, and you follow him."

"And?"

"Tonight is the night; follow him to wherever he's going. If you get the shot, take it. If you don't, I'm going to be waiting for him in that alley just outside his garage when he returns."

Camp jumped out of the Cadillac and knocked on the roof.

Kai was off, peeling rubber around the corner to catch up with Cooley. Camp strolled in the opposite direction from the Cooley house. On the cross street of the next block, he climbed into an old silver Chevy pickup. The back was full of rakes, shovels, hoes, and brooms. There was a mound of tree debris covered with a tarp. Consistent with his crappy appearance, Camp looked like a grimy junkyard worker or bootleg landscape laborer.

At the very bottom of the tarp and tree debris, wrapped in an oilcloth, was a .45-caliber Colt revolver. It looked like something from an old western or gangster movie.

Camp had filed the serial numbers off years ago. He cleaned and serviced it personally. He used it because it didn't lock or jam. He had Glocks, Rugers, and Berettas, but he never fully trusted them. He figured if he couldn't correct the situation with six shots of .45-caliber lead, then it probably wasn't correctable. He jumped in the old Silverado and drove down the alley, getting into position a few yards from the rear of the Cooleys' garage.

## Chapter Eighteen

*The Big Boo Classic Step Show* involved all the nationally noted black fraternities and sororities. It was being televised live on TV1 and BET, with blow-by-blow announcers. The scoring system was explained to people watching at home. The judges included presidents from several organizations and recording artists known for their dance moves. While most step shows took the audience back to their days in college, *The Big Boo Classic Step Show* was designed to introduce HBU step shows to the world at large. It felt similar to shows like *World of Dance* and *America's Got Talent*. The judges would score and provide commentary between acts.

There were three categories: team step, individual step, and coed stepping, where select fraternities and sororities teamed up for a single performance.

The first round was the challenge round. The top two performers from each category moved to the championship round.

For the next three hours, Atlanta forgot about death, protests, and politics. Choppy and Chunky Wells were in the crowd, cheering. They were Kappa men, so they wore crimson and cream from head to toe.

The Kappa men came out stepping with their iconic canes and tailored sports coats. Their routine had the smoothness of a Motown act.

They were followed by the men of Omega Psi Phi. Their step routine was highlighted by boundless jumps and landing in powerful boot stomps. They needed no music and no costumes, wearing their skin-tight purple t-shirt, black jeans, and gold boots.

Alpha Phi Alpha's step routine had a historical theme. The brothers started in ragged slave garb, and with some slick offstage quick changes, they moved to white t-shirts and jeans and then into long tail tuxedo coats and top hats.

Phi Beta Sigma came out with a ninja set, recreating a martial arts movie scene, with kicks and stunt fighting interspersed throughout the step routine.

The Iota Phi Theta men had a high-energy performance with their signature skip/step/clap routine.

The ladies also went big production.

Delta Sigma Theta presented a Flash of Red. Their routine was a powerful step routine in the costume of the female warriors from the motion picture *Black Panther*.

Sigma Gamma Rho had a retro theme. They came out in wide-leg jumpsuits and stage smoke. They were very athletic, and their step routine was the most powerful of all the sororities. Halfway through the routine, the stage went to black light, and the jumpsuits had an eerie glow. It was a nice effect.

Zeta Phi Beta did their step routine dressed like famous girl bands: TLC, En Vogue, Destiny's Child, and Salt-N-Pepa.

Alpha Kappa Alpha closed out the first half of the show. They came out in pink tailored business suits that accented all the right spots. Their routine started demurely, with more choreographed dance moves. Then, halfway through, the suits were ripped away, leaving the ladies in tight-fitting green athletic shorts and t-shirts. They stomped up a sweat to make it worth it.

TruLuv was amongst the judges, and once again, he was in his element, laughing and joking with everyone. He became known as the easy judge, giving out too many tens for the taste of the rest of the judges, but he didn't care because the crowd loved his enthusiasm.

During the first intermission, I found Teri talking to some of her Delta sisters.

"When did you get here?" I asked.

"Just now; I was on my way to find you but had to holla," she said and then gave an "OOO-OOP" call that only Deltas understand and answer. Her sisters responded. That was followed with an AKA "Skee-Wee" call and response from some ladies dressed in pink and green in the opposite corner of the backstage area. I pulled her to the side so I could hear myself talk.

"And?"

"And what, Darryl?"

"Stop playing," I said. "You lit out of the house like your shoes were on fire. You were on to something."

I knew Teri hated being so obvious, but I was right. It must have taken everything she had not to call me from the hospital and from Elliott Street Cafe

"Where is Bobby Sr.?" she asked.

"Managing the operatives from the control vehicle in the parking lot," I explained.

From our surveillance vehicle and it's connectivity to our operatives, Bobby Sr. could manage an entire operation. In addition, he could maintain exterior containment. This had happened in real time a while back.

Early last year, some thieves executed a grab and dash of jewelry at an event we were securing. Imagine the thieves' surprise as they pushed through the rear door after evading us and there was Bobby Sr. in his iBOT robotic chair, elevated to six feet tall and aiming a short-stock Winchester rifle right at them. It was all she wrote.

The intermission at the step show ended, so we had to hold Teri's news. The night ended with a very smooth step performance by some of the older brothers and sisters. It was called "Classic Step – Takin' 'Em to School." I do not think there was a person under fifty on the floor, but you could not tell by the soul in the clap or the power in the stomp. The men were in loose-fitting white dress shirts with full sleeves and black sharkskin slacks. The ladies were actually in knee-length sleeveless dresses in small floral print.

They started doing a couples steppin' exhibition to "Ain't No Stoppin' Us Now" by McFadden and Whitehead. That got the older crowd to clappin'. Then, at the end of the first chorus, every couple broke into a smooth but powerful coed step routine to James Brown's "Papa Got a Brand New Bag." It was as classy and stylish as anything you would see on

Broadway.

As the crowd started to leave, I found my way next to TruLuv, who was signing autographs and congratulating a famous rapper from Atlanta on the success of his latest motion picture release about fast cars, big guns, and international espionage.

I took the time to conduct roll call with the team. Teri and her operatives were between my position and the exit. They had eye contact on TruLuv and me. Bobby Sr. was on surveillance at the rear entrance.

I was looking over the crowd for a glimpse of the twins or the Ferguson group. I didn't see them.

"Field Unit Alpha, report in," I called into my communicator. Field Unit Alpha was the code for the operatives that were following Chunky and Choppy Wells and the Ferguson Force for Change. There was no answer for several seconds as I continued looking over the crowd. I heard Teri repeat my call for Field Unit Alpha through the communicator.

The cell phone on my hip vibrated repeatedly, like when you get weather warnings or Amber Alerts. I checked it. It was two separate texts from Bobby Jr. and the operatives to the rest of us.

"911 911 FIELD UNIT AND TWINS ABOUT TO BE AMBUSHED BY WHITE GUYS. ALLEY NEAR APARTMENTS AT JACKSON AND IRWIN STREETS. GOTTA STAY UNDERCOVER BUT SEND HELP ASAP BEFORE FIELD UNIT ALPHA HAS TO USE EXTREME MEANS."

As I looked up from my phone, I saw Teri and her detail moving through the crowd towards me. She was holding up her phone, showing she had received the same text.

"Take over for TruLuv with one operative. I will take the rest and get out to the spot," I said, pointing to the operatives I wanted to follow me.

"Bobby Sr. is ready behind the wheel out back. Hurry, Darryl!" Teri said, looking worried.

I moved through the crowd, with two operatives in front of me and two behind, looking like business. The crowd parted with little trouble.

When we reached the rear entrance, Bobby Sr. was behind the wheel of the black vehicle he used as his control center. The side door was open; the operatives got in back. I hopped in the front passenger seat.

"I got the transponder signals locked in!" he said as he flexed the hand accelerator, and we were gone.

We moved through the parking lot car and foot traffic, blowing the horn and flashing our lights. I continued to call Field Unit Alpha, praying they were not answering for reasons other than being in full combat engagement.

Bobby Sr. made a sharp right out of the parking lot onto Peachtree Center Avenue NE, heading north. Then we took the third left onto John Wesley Dobbs, heading east. Bobby Sr. continued to flash his headlights and blow his horn, and we fractured a few traffic regulations as we bogarted our way through several four-way stops. In a few blocks, we were in a residential neighborhood in mid-gentrification. At some point, Dobbs became Irwin St.

There were rows of old hulking houses, dark, ghostly structures with no lights, interspersed with major construction of single- and multiple-unit homes illuminated like it was midafternoon.

We slowed to a crawl.

"They are close. On your side of the street, Lem," Bobby Sr. said as he put on the bright lights. I lowered the passenger side window and put the Maglite Xenon LED flashlight on every house, shining in windows, on driveways, and up and down the streets.

The vehicle was whisper quiet as we listened as hard as we looked for something to give us a clue where they were. I looked over at the tablet screen showing the transponder location. We were right on top of them. The twins should have been within twenty feet of my car door. I fought to keep my panic down and told myself to stay focused on the process.

Headlights turned from a side street and headed our way. It was moving, a small sedan with three or four men inside. I checked the transponder read. The icons were in the same spot.

"It's not them, Lem. Not sure who they are, but it's not the twins or Bobby Jr.," Bobby Sr. said with a sigh.

Then I heard it. Voices. Arguing. Curses and the grunts associated with the early stages of fighting.

"Stop here! We're on foot from here," I said, already opening my door. I crossed to the other side of the street, following the sound of the voices. The operatives were out of the vehicle, following behind me, guns drawn.

"No shooting unless I make the call," I whispered. The last thing I needed was for the twins or Bobby Jr. to get hit by friendly fire.

We moved down the sidewalk. Just past two more houses, there was an open field partially illuminated by a streetlight at the corner. We could make out curses and distinct words.

"Double time," I whispered and broke into a soft-footed jog.

Hiding in front of the last house, I peeked around the left side and saw them.

The twins and two operatives were surrounded by about seven Caucasian men. It appeared to be some kind of standoff. Chunky, the tall twin, was face to face with a tattooed, muscled, pale-skinned bruiser with a bald head and red beard, each of them holding fistfuls of each other's jacket. One operative, his gun drawn, was shielding Choppy behind him. The other operative had one of the white guys in a chokehold. There were others on both sides doing a lot of talking but not moving much.

I sent the three short text vibrations to all the operatives, the universal signal we'd set.

As slick as we'd rehearsed it, the two operatives in the scuffle changed their stance. The operative holding his captive in a chokehold shoved him into his red-bearded partner. This freed Chunky, who was pulled back next to his brother under the protection of the other operative. As both operatives raised their guns, and before anyone knew what was happening, my team brought up the rear.

"All right, everybody freeze!" I said. "We don't want to shoot, so don't be stupid."

Hands went up on both sides. One of my operatives holstered and started extracting members of the Ferguson Force for Change. About that time, Choppy noticed it was me; he started to speak, but I motioned for him to be silent.

"You ain't police! This don't concern you!" Red Beard said.

"Nope, not the police but just trying to even things up. We got five black guys and, what, about ten white guys with sticks and chains?"

"Just having a friendly conversation with the bros," Red Beard said.

"Yeah, right. Well, this is a done deal," I said, motioning for the operatives to move the twins and their friends out to the vehicle. Three of the operatives and I kept guns on our friends.

As we backed away, we noticed one white guy was cursing and coughing; he was the one who had been in the chokehold. As he straightened and turned to the light, I realized it was a scruffy Bobby Jr.

## Chapter Nineteen

David Cooley was feeling better. After spending some time alone at Grace and Mercy Catholic Church, he met Father Burke, a kindly, gentle giant who stood about six feet six inches tall and weighed three hundred pounds. He was local, speaking with a Georgia accent, and had graduated from North Atlanta High School. He'd attended this same church as a child.

Father Burke had a way of getting people to talk just by listening. It was exactly what David Cooley needed. They didn't discuss God or religion. They just discussed life, specifically David's life.

Two hours later, when evening mass started, David felt obligated to stay. He sat in the back of the sanctuary. He still didn't know what he believed in, but he just closed his eyes and let the calming feeling of the words and the music and atmosphere flow over him. He didn't think about the case, the media, or his upcoming trial.

After service, he got up to leave, but he was stopped by a couple of parishioners who recognized who he was. One elderly gentleman showed David his old credentials. He'd worn the shield for Atlanta Metro up until the mid-1980s. He told stories of working during the Wayne Williams Atlanta child murders of 1979–1981.

David felt more positive than he ever had. There were people who did not know him, but they chose to believe him. They weren't anti-Butta, but they were still pro-police until proven guilty. It told a much different story than what had been seen on television news or social media sites. He felt for the first time since the shooting that he would have a shot at being heard.

The congregation was departing, leaving David and Father Burke on the front steps of the church. David had received invitations to a number of homes that evening, but he knew he had been away from Anousha and Daria long enough. However, he stuck around to thank Father Burke for listening and keeping him sane.

He walked past the last few parishioners to the big cheerful priest. David wasn't a hugger, but he couldn't help himself. He embraced Father Burke, who responded in kind. He felt the warmth coming through his robes.

Then the warmth began to drip onto David's face.

Father Burke's arms tightened around him in an unnatural manner. He looked up, and half the priest's face was a bloody, explosive mess.

"Oh God!" David said reflexively. He stepped back, but Father Burke held him tight. David fell backward, pulling the big priest onto the church steps as three more silent shots blistered the front façade of the church. Sharp chips of stone flew in all directions.

There was a scream behind him. Lying on the steps, David wrenched himself from Father Burke's embrace and turned to see. An elderly woman with a rich silver mane of hair was lying back against her husband. There was a bloody hole in her chest and cuts on her face.

*Was she shot? Or just cut by the stone?* he thought.

She was screaming repeatedly, in pain and shock. Her husband was holding her, speechless. The last few churchgoers ran for cover, some for their cars, some in the nearby shrubbery.

David felt hands pulling on him. It was the retired police officer.

"Son, get off these steps before they shoot the lot of us!" he shouted as additional shots pinged off the steps and front of the building.

David made a move towards Father Burke, who was lying diagonally across three steps, his blood running to the sidewalk below.

*Is he still breathing?* David thought as he crawled to the priest. He reached the edge of Father Burke's robe, and three more bullets – pulck, pulck, pulck – exploded inches from his hand and head, shattering the granite all around him. David closed his eyes protectively and felt his face sting with hundreds of tiny cuts from the rock shards. He scrambled back, and the retired cop pulled him the rest of the way, to the left side of the steps. They found a cripple wall and ducked behind it, between the trash bin and the wall of the church.

David could barely hear anything except his heartbeat in his ear. He listened for more shots but heard none. He and the elderly ex-cop stared into each other's faces. The smell of rotten trash and blood was thick in the air. He handed David a handkerchief and motioned to his face. David gave his cheek a wipe. The white fabric was streaked with red. He continued to wipe until the distant sirens drew near.

Kai had lost and re-found David Cooley several times in the myriad of turns he'd made through the East Atlanta area. By a stroke of dumb luck, she found his car parked outside a church. It made sense. A man in trouble reaching out for divine help.

Surveying the surrounding neighborhood, she found one of many multi-story reconstructions, manifestations of Atlanta's growing wave of gentrification. This one was half finished, three stories tall, with open windows that faced the church. She casually walked past the church, hoping to put eyes on Cooley to make sure he hadn't switched the car or proceeded someplace on foot. On the third walk around the block, she ventured up to the door, opening it slightly. She saw Cooley talking to the priest.

She felt an unnatural streak of guilt, like an instrument of evil lurking just outside the confines of the Lord's house. She laughed at herself as she tiptoed away. This was the guy who'd shot Butta. 'Nuf said.

She waited patiently across the street in the bare-boned shell of a house. She camped on the plywood floor with rifle and rounds. She set up the Barret M82 sniper rifle with a Griffin suppressor. She would take the shot as soon as possible.

Then, over two hours later, she got her shot. She thought about leaving when people showed up for evening mass, but she didn't want to be seen. She called Camp and gave him an update. He was still holding up in the alley in case Cooley returned.

Then mass let out. People spilled out onto the steps, including the big red-headed priest. Then there was Cooley. He was actually smiling and shaking hands with old people out on the steps.

*Smile now, muthafucka*, she thought as she sighted him through the scope. *I'm a blow that grin clean off your face.*

She'd actually set up the tripod and rifle two feet from the opening, the tip of the suppressor just beyond but unnoticeable in the dim light.

Kai had killed at least seven people in her life. She had never been caught because, above all, she was patient. She did not talk, and she had a plan. She had been in that window this long; she would wait a while longer to get the best shot. She would only get one chance.

Twenty minutes later, the crowd was thinning. She had hoped to get Cooley alone, but a few witnesses wouldn't stop her. She could lay down the shot, break down the rifle and the tripod, and then walk out the back of the half-finished house, down the alley to the Cadillac. She had a secret compartment in the rear storage area for the firearms.

When there were fewer than ten people on the steps, Kai found David Cooley in her scope. She would take him soon. Just as soon as he separated himself from the others.

*Won't be long n . . .* she was saying to herself when she heard it. The SPHLIT, SPHLIT, SPHLIT of bullets through a silencer, followed by the screams of people on the steps.

She jumped to her feet and pulled her Glock. The shooter had to be near; she could hear the shots. She heard two more and saw the pops on the front of the church.

She jumped down to the rifle and sighted through the scope. She looked right and left until she found Cooley embraced by the priest. Then she saw the clergyman's face.

Three more shots, and more screams from the front of the church.

This wasn't the plan. She broke her gear down and stored it in the case. Leading with her Glock, she went down the rear steps with no incident. She saw no one and heard nothing. She ran across the backyard and down the alley. She heard more screams from the church.

When she got to her Cadillac, she checked to make sure the streets were empty and stowed the rifle. She willed her body to move casually as she got behind the wheel. She started the engine and waited thirty seconds while her heart beat like an 808 drum. After that, she slowly eased into traffic, moving away from the church. Continuing south with no turns, she watched police and ambulance units speeding in the opposite direction. She maintained her bored, apathetic expression, looking forward like all the other drivers. After another mile, she pulled into the parking lot of a Tin Lizzy's Restaurant.

"Camp, things are fucked!" she said when he answered. She rattled off what had happened outside the church.

"Who was it?" Camp asked.

"I have no idea."

"Did they get Cooley?"

"Shit, I don't know; I got the hell out of there. They hit the priest, maybe one other civilian."

Silence.

"Camp!"

"What?"

"Man, what the fuck? Did you hire another shooter? Someone to hunt Cooley?"

"No, and if I did, I would have said so."

"Then who is this?"

"Maybe a vigilante," Camp theorized. "Black folks all over the city hate his ass."

"Nooo, I don't think so," Kai said. "This felt . . . professional."

"How?"

"They were using a suppressor, a good one. I could tell by the sound. Plus, I think they were set up in the same house that I posted myself in, just on the third floor. They either got up there without my notice or they were there before me. That means they heard me on the second floor but did not let me know they were there."

"I see," Camp said, sounding preoccupied. Or maybe he was thinking through what she was saying.

"Well, I don't see. Why would someone do that? Camp, who else is putting professional muscle on the street to off

Cooley?"

SILENCE

"Camp . . . ? Camp?"

## Chapter Twenty

Camp Butterfield had been locked in on the Cooley home. He was waiting for Kai to call him back with news that the deed was done. Cooley would be dead like his cousin. He had a police scanner listening to calls. He wanted to be far away from the city when the news hit.

As day turned to night, he could see into some of the rear windows where the light was on. He saw Anousha for the first time in over a year. She was sitting at what looked like the dining room table, reading something. She looked like he remembered her. Beautiful, classy, like she was descended from royalty. He also saw Daria, the daughter, the kid he hadn't known about when they'd been together.

Back then, they had agreed not to ask too many background questions. He had assumed it was because there were parts of his life she should not know about. He was a gangster; he did unlawful things and associated with known criminals.

He'd never imagined she'd been hiding just as much, if not more, than him. He had missed her when she'd left. She was the only person he dealt with who was not in the business of crime. He could be himself with her. He could be Marques with her. Watching her now in what appeared to be one of the bedrooms, he wondered how he could still feel the way he did given she wasn't who she said she was. His phone rang.

Just as he answered it, there was the sound of glass breaking.

He looked around to see where it had come from while Kai was talking about something going wrong. Cooley wasn't dead, but someone else was shot. He was trying to understand what Kai was saying when . . .

KRA-VOOM!

The Cooley kitchen windows exploded with flames and smoke. Before Camp realized what was happening, flames and smoke were spreading all across the interior of the house. He could see Anousha in the bedroom windows. She had heard it as well. She looked scared and confused.

Hanging up on Kai, he moved on instinct. The old truck screamed into motion as he slammed it into gear and jammed the gas pedal. He drove to the end of the alley and whipped the wheel left onto the side street. Then he took another left onto the street in front of the Cooley house.

*Where is the patrol?* he wondered.

He parked in front of the house in the wrong direction. The Cooley house was ablaze, flames coming from several windows and the opening where the front door used to be. The street was empty. Camp thought he saw taillights speeding away two blocks up the street. He couldn't see the make or model.

He ran to the front of the house on automatic pilot, knowing he had to do something but not sure what.

Then he saw little Daria standing in the foyer hall. He was in front of the fiery door front, and he could see her standing there looking small and lost. She was in her pajamas and holding a Mickey Mouse doll.

"Daria, where are you, baby?" Anousha's voice called out over the crackle of the fire and building wood falling from the burning. Another window exploded outward, and it brought Camp out of his quandary.

He held his breath as he ran through the fire and over the front door lying on the porch and into the house. His shoes felt hot. He looked down and saw smoke blooming up from his feet and flames working their way up his pant legs. He beat out the fire with his bare hands.

When he reached Daria, she seemed confused and sleepy. Camp picked her up. She felt as light as a pillow.

"Don't be afraid, honey. I won't let nothing happen to you," he said because he didn't know what else to say.

"I was just getting some water before bed," she explained. "Then I saw the man and all this fire."

She was right; the fire was getting higher. The smoke was thick. Camp looked around for the way to the kitchen. He found the half-bath first. Holding Daria in his left arm, he snatched decorative towels off the rack and began to drench them in water in the vanity sink. Daria was starting to nod on his shoulder. She smelled like a baby.

"No, no, little one, you got to stay awake," he explained.

"Where is my mama?" she asked, tearful emotion coming into her throat.

"I don't know, but I am going to get you out of here first. Then I promise to get your mama."

"Are you a fireman?" she asked.

"Um . . . no, well, kind of. What's your name?" Camp asked, trying to keep her talking. She told him. He stood Daria on the closed toilet seat. Then he soaked the towels so they were still dripping water. He draped one over his head and motioned like it was long, flowing hair. Daria giggled groggily.

"Now your turn," Camp said. He placed the other wet towel over her head. She shivered, and her eyes widened.

"That's cold," she said.

"Ok, Daria, we're going outside to wait for the rest of the fireman and Mama," Camp explained. She nodded with the towel dripping over her small frame. He picked her up again. The towel was wet and cold, and she shivered again.

"Oh, honey, close your eyes and keep them closed until I tell you to open them. She did as he instructed.

As they moved back into the hallway, the flames were still growing on everything, but the white smoke was solid. Camp could not see more than six inches in front of him. There was a smell of burning plastic. He heard electrical arcing from compromised outlets. He also heard, more than saw, wood burning. He realized he had not heard Anousha in some time.

Daria coughed repeatedly.

"Eyes closed, kiddo," Camp said, and he pulled the wet towel over her face.

Then he moved through the smoke. He tried to bend to get lower, but it was hard with Daria in his arms. At first, he moved quickly and almost tripped on burning wood in his path. He caught himself and slowly shuffled the rest of the way. He bumped into partially burned walls and had to blindly alter his steps around two more mounds of debris. After two minutes that seemed like two hours, he smelled fresh air and successfully followed his nose. When he reached the front yard, he pulled the towel back. Daria opened her eyes and began coughing again.

"Where is Mama?" she asked between coughs.

"Right away," Camp said. He looked around for someplace to leave her. He settled on the front seat of his old truck.

He put the wet towel around his head, mouth, and nose. He sized up the smoky wreck of a house and then ran inside. Once past the demolished foyer, he dropped to his hands and knees and headed down the hall towards the rooms where he'd last seen her. He could feel splinters and glass digging into his palms and his knees.

He called her name through the towel, but he got no response. He started to think the worst but forced himself to focus.

When he looked in all the rooms and hadn't found her, he circled back to the room from which he'd seen her in the window. He almost tripped over her feet, which were extending just past the far side of the bed. She was unconscious on the floor.

"Anousha!" he shouted between coughs. He shook her, but she was out.

He could just make out a siren in the distance. He didn't

have much time. As if on automatic pilot, he scooped her up and was soon going down the hall. Keeping his eyes down, he moved around the debris with better agility.

The sirens seemed to be close. All Camp thought was that he couldn't be here. Standing on the front lawn, he worried about a neighbor capturing his efforts on video. The patrol could not be far away. He thought about leaving Anousha and Daria lying in the front yard, but it would take too long. Fire engines would be coming around the corner any minute. Throwing Anousha over his shoulder, he opened the passenger-side door and lowered her onto the seat. Daria scooted over but was clearly scared.

"She's just asleep, sweetie; the smoke made her tired," Camp said, wondering where he'd gotten all this touchy-feely kid talk. "We will wake her up later."

Daria looked dubious and just nodded. She was on her knees in the front seat.

He rounded the front of the truck, looking frantically over his body for his keys. Then he saw them still in the ignition. He started the old truck and made ready to peel out. Then he thought, *That would look like a guy who just torched a house.*

He calmly placed the truck in drive and forced himself to ease away from the curb. At the next corner, he could hear the sirens coming from the right. He eased into a left turn onto the side street. Then he took a right two streets over from the Cooley house. With each mile, he felt calmer and calmer. No one followed him all the way out to South Fulton County.

## Chapter Twenty-one

After securing the twins and their friends in the vehicle, I kept my temper and buttoned down my voice until we got back to the base house. The twins and their friends had enough good sense to follow my lead and remain silent.

During the drive back, Teri reported that TruLuv was secure and at the base.

The driveway extends up the right side of the house and opens onto a rear courtyard that curves around to double garage doors on the lower level of the house. We pulled in front of the garage doors, and one of them opened.

"Chunky and Choppy, I want to see you and your friends inside in fifteen minutes," I said and got out of the car before they could say something to piss me off further.

I found TruLuv in the small sitting room at the front of the house. I plopped down in an oversized leather chair. A Booker's bourbon on the rocks appeared in front of me. TruLuv was at the other end of the drink.

"I know it was a scary situation, Pop," he said after about five minutes and after I'd taken a few sips of my drink. He sat next to me with a drink of his own. "But don't be too hard on them."

"You weren't there," I said. "This was seconds away from going bad. Real bad. And it's not over."

"What do you mean?" TruLuv asked, taking a sip of his drink and fighting a grimace.

"We pulled our weapons tonight, an action that should be reported to the police by us and probably will be reported by that group of troublemakers," I explained.

"But they were asshole troublemakers," TruLuv said.

"Then it begs the question as to why we didn't get the police involved," Teri explained as she strolled into the room.

"It was life and death; the twins would have been hurt or worse if you had waited on the police," TruLuv rationalized.

"Then we should have been better in our security so it would not have come to this," I explained. "In a few minutes, I am going to find out why we didn't."

"Any word from Bobby Jr.?" Teri asked.

"Maybe he has reached out to his father. He did a pretty good job of holding his cover," I explained.

Bobby Sr. and Bobby Jr. had a series of texts they used to communicate in code. The texts appeared to be flirtatious statements from a female admirer. Each was code for a specific message. Bobby Jr.'s responses were equally coded responses to the flirts.

"I didn't even know it was him until he started coughing from the chokehold," I said.

"Chokehold?" Teri asked.

"It was one of us holding him; he was fine," I said.

Taking a final sip from the Booker's, I looked over at TruLuv and smiled. "Man, why are you wasting my liquor? You know you don't drink."

TruLuv just shrugged and smiled.

"You trying your New Age love magic on me?" I laughed. "Don't worry. I've known those kids most of their lives. I'm just glad they're alive."

"You was thinkin' about Alexis?" TruLuv said.

I just sighed, shook my head, and bit down on a cube of seasoned ice.

Alexis LaVette had been a sweet girl and an amazing singer. On a crazy night in New Orleans, she'd left her hotel room against my direction and washed up dead in the shallow waters off Belle Chase. I knew she'd gone out on her own, but she'd still died on our watch.

We went into the rear ballroom, which served as our command center. The twins and their friends were sitting on the sofas, their faces and fingers glued to their phones. The two operatives assigned to them were securing equipment and trying to look busy. I motioned for them to come over to the sitting area. I patted both of them on the shoulders to indicate I wasn't in a killing mode. I could see them relax, which is what I wanted. Better for me to get at the truth. We were all sitting in an oblong circle, the twins and friends on the couch, the two operatives in the loveseat, Teri in the matching oversized chair, and I in a chair pulled from the dining room.

"I just want to know what happened tonight. I promise not to preach if you promise not to lie. Whoever wants to start."

"Well, I mean no disrespect, Mr. Lem, but I don't need to be here," said one of the friends. "You not the police, and. . . I'm a grown man, and—"

"Man, shut up," Chunky said, cutting him off. "This man saved our asses tonight. You want to leave? Get to walking or call an Uber. Hope them cracka white boys ain't still out there looking for us."

Silence from Mr. "Grown Ass Man." I motioned for one of the twins to start.

"We left the step show early," Chunky said. "We told the security we were looking for an after party."

"Yeah, but that wasn't true," I guessed.

"Uh, right," Chunky said. "We were meeting some folks."

"Who?" I asked.

"Some fellow Nupes that work for the county."

"Why?"

"They reached out to us," Chunky said.

"For what?"

"They said they had something for us."

"And. . ." I prodded.

"We met up with them, and then these white guys came from out of nowhere."

I sighed and looked at Teri, who sat there with her lips folded under with aggravation.

"I'm going to go another way on this," I said. "I know you all are over twenty-one, but I will still call all your parents tonight and put you on a plane tomorrow if I don't get more than I'm getting."

Chunky started to talk again, but I held up my right hand and pointed to the operatives sitting to my left. They were Michael Johnson and Murphy Moore. They went by Johnson and Murphy. Johnson was six foot four and slim, with caramel-brown skin and a bald head, a Boris Kodjoe body double. Murphy was shorter, all muscle, with a "don't fuck with me" countenance. Johnson did the talking.

"We followed the group out of the event, maintaining loose coverage like instructed. Then short twin over there came to us saying they were going to a meeting. Murph and I thought it was funny, so we tightened our coverage, actually walking with them instead of following."

I nodded. Teri leaned forward, wondering where this was going.

"We kept walking almost a mile, twisting and turning through neighborhoods. We thought about sending Murph back for one of the vehicles, but the twins kept saying we were close. Eventually, a car pulls up next to us in the middle of the block. One of them makes the Kappa call, and they start talking."

"Nupes?" Teri asked the twins. They nodded and started to talk, but she cut them off. "What next, Johnson?"

"We all stood there, talking for a couple of minutes. Whispering, actually. We couldn't hear what they were saying. Then someone started calling the twins by their names from the direction we came."

"The white boys?" I asked. "You knew them, Chunky?"

"No, but I think they knew us from the day at McDonald's. You know, social media."

"Right, you two are famous," I said with a sigh. "Go on, Johnson."

"I could see we were outnumbered. I told everyone to move up the street double time, but the twins were still going back and forth with the people in the car. By the time they finished, the rednecks were less than a block away. The car peeled off, and we ran for it. We didn't get far before we were surrounded."

"The car, was it a small import?" I asked, remembering the sedan full of people that had sped past us.

Nods all around.

"That it?" I asked the entire group.

They all nodded again except Murphy, who shook his head.

"The twins got a package," he explained. "From the people in the car. That's why they took so long. Convincing them that the package would stay confidential."

I turned back to the twins and their friends.

"Well, what was it? What did they give you?" I asked.

They looked at each other as if making their minds up. They reminded me of the game show *To Tell The Truth*, when contestants would look at each other surreptitiously to misdirect the audience. Finally, Choppy reached behind him and under his shirt. He pulled a tan envelope eight inches by fourteen inches and folded lengthwise.

"Were you hiding that in your underwear?" Teri asked incredulously.

"The backside of his underwear, near his ass," Murphy said, making a face as if something smelled.

The room broke out into laughter.

Choppy placed it in my hand. I unfolded and opened the envelope. I felt Teri walk around to the back of my chair so she could read over my shoulder.

"Preliminary autopsy findings – Shawn J. Butterfield," I read on the first page.

"This is the coroner's report on Butta's death?" Teri asked.

"The first draft," Choppy said.

"Who gave you this?" I asked.

"And why?" Teri asked.

"We got some fraternity brothers working in the coroners' office. They care about making sure the truth doesn't get covered over by the machine trying to clear that dirty cop," Choppy explained. "When they start changing the facts over the course of the case, this may find its way into the press."

I just looked at them all, nodding with confidence and

bravado. I wondered if I had been this naïve when I'd been their age. I knew I had been that cocky, which is why I was able to keep from strangling every one of them for being stupid.

Teri was explaining all the laws they'd just broken. Her fiancé, Lucious Barnett, had come up in the St. Louis district attorney's office. She had heard more court stories than bedtime stories. That, along with her time with the police department, meant she had more than enough knowledge to know of what she spoke.

I took this time to read over the report. Most of it was standard language. Shawn had succumbed to a single gunshot wound. The ballistics test was not finished yet, but I wasn't sure it would matter. The bullet that had killed Shawn Butterfield had broken into pieces.

"So can we leave, Mr. Lem? I just want to go to sleep," one of the friends asked. He hadn't said much all night. He looked tired. He was a follower who had been promised a night of excitement and had gotten this.

"I don't know if anybody should be leaving yet," said a voice from behind us. It was Bobby Sr. "Check the news on your phones. There have been some developments."

## Chapter Twenty-two

We watched the news explode around the city about the attempted murder of Officer David Cooley.

There had been a shooting at a small church where Cooley had attended mass. The priest had been shot in the face and had to undergo emergency surgery. He was in a coma but was expected to live. There were a number of other parishioners injured from flying brick debris and from falls associated with fleeing the gunfire.

The saddest part of the news was the death of Melba Gernst, seventy-eight years old. The grandmother of eight, and great-grandmother of three, had been struck in the chest by one of the bullets. She'd suffered a heart attack while in surgery and succumbed to her injuries.

Cooley had not been struck. He had some cuts and scrapes from fleeing the gunfire and a sprained ankle.

At the exact same time, David Cooley's house had been firebombed, and his wife and child were missing. It had happened during the shift change of the patrol, who had left before their replacement had come. There was major structural damage to the front of the home and smoke and water damage throughout. The water damage had come from the fire department in their attempt to make sure the fire was extinguished. At any rate, the Cooley home was uninhabitable. David Cooley was being kept in a secret location.

Among their persons of interest, the police listed Marques

Campbell Butterfield, Shawn's cousin and a well-known drug dealer.

When the twins and their friends saw the coverage, they chose to spend the night at the base house. We had three spare bedrooms.

I felt it was time to figure out our next moves. Bobby Sr., Teri, and I met back in the kitchen around the same center island. It was not my idea, but TruLuv insisted on being included in the briefing. After all, he was paying the bills on this trip.

"I'm not sure what to believe," I said. "However, things are escalating, and we need to be on alert in terms of our protection of the twins and our client."

"So, you think Camp Butterfield did all this?" TruLuv asked.

"It would make perfect sense," I said, "but the signature feels wrong."

"Signature?" TruLuv asked.

"This was a coordinated attack," Teri explained. "Very unlike your typical street criminal, who prefers a single frontal attack, usually a drive-by."

"However, our intel from the local cops shows Camp Butterfield is not typical. He is careful, patient, and not prone to mistakes," I explained. "His second-in-command, a woman named Cadillac Kai Davis, is linked to at least four unsolved murders and has a reputation for being an expert with firearms."

"But then she wouldn't have missed so horribly," TruLuv

surmised.

"Exactly," I said.

"But that doesn't mean they didn't do it. No one's perfect," Bobby Sr. said. I nodded my agreement.

"Then there was the firebomb at his house. Why do it if Cooley was not there?" Teri asked.

"And that story about the patrol leaving early because the replacement was nearby?" I said.

"And another sloppy job of it," Bobby Sr. noted.

"And where the hell is Cooley's wife and child?" I asked no one in particular.

The room was quiet for several seconds. I wanted to keep my focus narrow, on the protection of my client and the young politicos sleeping upstairs. I wanted no part of the Shawn Butterfield/David Cooley case. It was becoming fractured, like these cases always do. I couldn't rule out some self-appointed vigilante group. I thought of the New Revolutionaries and made a mental note to call Captain Sayles in the morning.

The problem was TruLuv. I could tell from the look on his face that the violence surrounding this case had not deterred him one bit. He seemed more determined than ever to be involved in it. So, if my son was going to stay in this, I had to stay in this. In for a penny, in for a pound.

"You see why it wasn't a good idea to reach out to Camp Butterfield?" I asked him. TruLuv nodded and looked like he wanted to say something. I motioned for him to speak.

"We need to keep Cooley alive," he said flatly.

"Ok," I said, not expecting that to come out of his mouth.

"Lem, at the end of the day, we need to stop the killing," he explained. "Now, what happens if Cooley gets killed in revenge? The whole damn thing, Ferguson, Baltimore, and Atlanta gets tainted. That's what they want; plus, it gives them open season on us. Eye for an eye."

"So, now you're for David Cooley?" Bobby Sr. asked.

"Hell no, I want his ass prosecuted and in prison. I want him to be a symbol of what happens when you spill our blood. I don't want him to be a martyr for crooked police all over the country."

"What's Bobby Jr.'s status?" I asked his father.

"He's good," Bobby Sr. said, though his look of concern said otherwise. He said the young bigots still believed in him. The chokehold on him went a long way toward convincing the idiots that Junior is one of them."

"What's their next move?" I asked.

"He says half of them want to go to the police and file a report about the 'black maggots' that held them at gunpoint. The other half want to stay quiet; don't want the attention."

"We'll keep an eye out," I said as I looked around the kitchen island. When my eyes landed on Teri, I remembered.

"Hey, what was your news from earlier when you disappeared on us?" I said.

"Oh, the plot thickens, Darryl," Teri said with a self-satisfied smile. She never called me by my nickname. "It answers one of your questions. Where was Butta going that night he was shot?"

"Well?" I said.

"He was headed to see his girlfriend, the Birmingham A&M Big Boo Classic queen," Teri said, sitting back in her stool.

"Really? Shawn and Brianna?" TruLuv said. "He never said anything to me. Maybe it was recent."

"Not likely unless it was love at first sight," Teri said. "The queen is pregnant with Butta's baby."

The room went quiet again.

"How did you find this out?" I asked, knowing she couldn't wait to tell us. Teri had a steel trap of a mind for detail and deductive reasoning.

"Earlier today, Brianna collapsed at the Main Event Tent."

"I didn't see that; I was there all day," TruLuv said.

"Yeah, you were supposed to share the stage with her, but you were having too much fun with the other children," Teri said sardonically. "Now, let me finish. When Brianna collapsed, the ambulance responded. They asked her questions to test if she had a concussion. One was her address, 1404 Hunnicutt Street NW. Later on tonight, I was looking at the GPS screenshot where Butta was shot. He appeared to be going north across Ivan Allen Avenue. There are a number of apartment and condo complexes there, just east and north of the Atlanta Mission Shelter. As I looked over the map, I saw it, the street where Brianna lives with her mother. It was a stretch, but I thought it was worth a check."

"You went to her house?" I asked.

"No, the hospital," Teri said. "Turns out that they admitted the queen of the classic for observation overnight. She remembered me from the Culture Tent. She was embarrassed and didn't have much to say at first. Then I saw the sandwich wrapper from Elliott Street Cafe and literature on prenatal care on the nightstand next to her bed. She tried to deny it, but I promised not to go public."

Teri explained their conversation from her notes:

Teri: How far along are you?

Brianna: Just over three months.

T: How long have you been with Butta?

B: I know him as Shawn. I never used his performance name. We knew each other since we were kids. When we were in high school, he was always up to no good in my neighborhood. He would flirt a little here and there, but he knew better than to try anything serious. My head was fully focused on getting into school. I didn't have time for no thugs.

T: But something changed.

B: Yeah, last school year, I was walking across campus, and I saw some members of the band working on routines in the yard of their dorm. He was there. It took me a minute to recognize him. He was taller and had muscles and a nice smile. Don't get me wrong, I always thought he was cute, but before, he was always walking around trying to be hard, frowning, with a cigarette hanging from his lips. But damn, now he was fine!

T: So, you all started dating?

B: Not at first; he came at me hard, and I wanted him to, but the last time I saw him, he was posing as Camp Butterfield's bagman. I still wanted no part. He promised me that he was finished with that life, and he spent the rest of the semester proving it to me. He was in class, working out, and rehearsing hard with the drum majors. By the end of the school year, he had been named as one of the Roaring III.

T: So, he convinced you?

B (nodding while wiping away tears): We spent the entire summer together. We found jobs in Birmingham instead of going home. We shared a rental house with an older married couple. It felt like we were married too. I know that sounds silly, but we got along like that. We talked about moving in together permanently and made plans for after graduation. The couple we housed with were from Ghana; neither of us had thought about traveling outside the United States. Now we were looking into studying abroad.

T: You must have felt like a different person.

B: Have you ever had someone do that to you? You became a totally different person when you were with them? Anyway, fall semester started; we continued to make our plans. We didn't want a bunch of people up in our business, so we moved back into separate dorm rooms in separate buildings. Football season started, so Shawn was hella busy. I decided to run for homecoming queen, and I won.

T: So, you never saw each other. That can't be right.

B: Oh, no, we found times and places to be together. We were still friends with that married couple, and we housesat for them while they were away. Between studying, sneaking around with Shawn, and running for queen, I didn't notice that I missed two periods. Then this Big Boo Classic business started.

T: I get it. When did you know, and when did you tell Shawn?

B: About a month ago. I was so scared about what he might say.

T: He was happy?

B: He hugged me so hard it hurt. We were making plans to leave Atlanta together. Maybe start in Birmingham and finish school. Then there were all the plans we had made before, only now it would three instead of two.

T: So, why was he coming home to see you? Had you been sick?

B: Not really. I didn't want to be big and pregnant on the college campus. I altered my registration, picking up an online class curriculum, and split my time between my dorm room and my home. Shawn came to see me every time he got a chance. (Pause for tears.) He would always bring me a sandwich from Elliot's.

T: What about your family?

B: I had just told my mother the week before; she wasn't too happy. Then I told her that her grandchild was going to be a

Butterfield, and she freaked out. Shawn insisted on coming down for the weekend and meeting with her. Other weekends, we would spend with my cousin, who lives around the corner from me. Shawn wanted to make sure my mother knew ours was something real, something that would last. When he didn't show up and didn't answer his phone, she said some pretty awful things. Then the news came out the next morning about Shawn being shot. She was like everybody else, saying he had been working for his cousin and got killed.

T: She was pretty mad, huh?

B: Yeah, but more so scared. She told me not to tell anyone else. She hasn't slept since I told her. I've been worried sick and heartsick. I don't even know how to be without Shawn. I keep expecting to get one of his daydreaming texts about something he saw that made him think of me and the baby, his family.

T: What do you think she's scared of? The Butterfields?

B: I don't know. I guess. She mentioned some history between the Butterfields and the Daniels, but she wouldn't say anything more.


END OF NOTES


"We need to share this with the police," TruLuv said. His face was electric with rage and vindication. "This will put an end to all this speculation about Shawn being a thug, about him working for his cousin."

"We can't," Teri said. "I promised Brianna."

TruLuv started to respond. Then he just grunted in frustration and smacked his hand on the table.

"We will let the right people know," I said, "but we got to be careful."

"How so?" TruLuv asked.

"Like, what was the reason for all the secrecy?" Bobby Sr. said. "Even before the baby entered the picture, they kept this relationship a secret. There's more to this story; the sweet Brianna must have some idea."

"Also, we got another possibility on who shot Butta," I said.

"No, we know who shot Butta! It was Cooley," TruLuv said defiantly.

"Did he? Or was it someone tied to the Daniels family?" I said.

"Lem, now the Daniels are criminals?" TruLuv said.

"No, but there is more to this story, and if we are going to do what YOU want, put Butta's killer away, we got to close all the loose ends."

"Ok, what's our next move?" TruLuv asked.

"First, we are going to get some sleep," I said. "In the morning, we will get the twins and their friends off to a hard day's protesting with beefed-up protection. Then Bobby Sr. and I will have a conversation with Captain Sayles about tonight's event and ask him what he knows about criminal enemies."

"And what about me?" TruLuv asked.

I reached over and placed my hand on his shoulder, my face extra grim.

"You, my son, have rehearsal."

## Chapter Twenty-three

Earlier that night, Kai had maneuvered her way from the church, driving very slowly through the neighborhood after neighborhood. She dismantled her gun behind a strip mall in Lakewood Heights and switched license plates. Then she threw each part into six different sewer canals. Finally, she wound her way south and west to Camp's retreat in South Fulton County just off Camp Creek Parkway where it disappeared into the wilderness. Thinking they were safe, Kai was stunned to find Camp brooding, smelling like smoke, drinking again, and in the company of David Cooley's wife and kid.

Camp said they might need a doctor. They could send for Dr. Fingerlee a medical genius who had lost his practice and his teaching position at Emory when he'd become a too-frequent customer of Camp Butterfield. Kai and Camp had actually rehabbed him twice and set him up in business as physician to the criminal underworld of Atlanta.

The doctor came and went during the night. Everyone would live. They were scraped up, dehydrated, and exhausted. He left oxygen for them to use when they woke up. It would help clear smoke from their lungs.

Then Camp and Kai went into the garage and had it out. Kai told her story about what had happened at the church. Camp told his story about the firebombing.

"What the hell are you doing, Camp?"

"I couldn't leave 'em; the house was ablaze."

"But you got 'em out. Why bring them here?"

"It was the only move at the time."

"You could have just left."

"The girl saw my face. She could identify me."

He was right. Had he left them on the front yard and had the police found them, the kid's story would have made it seem like Camp had torched the house and pulled them out when he'd realized Cooley wasn't there.

"So, what happens when they wake up? Kidnapping comes with a life sentence, man."

"We didn't kidnap them, and she won't say that," Camp said with a drunk hiccup.

"Why? Cuz she still loves you?" Kai said sarcastically. "Wake up, fool. She was playing you; you two were playing each other. That wasn't love, and you know it."

"CK, we got bigger problems, like who did the shooting at the church and who torched the house? Who is trying to make it look like us going after Cooley and his family?"

"Well, I ain't told nobody," Kai said. "Has your auntie been talking?"

"To who?" Camp said incredulously. "She don't know nobody in the life."

"Well, somebody is making moves against us; they got us on the edge of a couple of graves, and they'll push us in unless we stop them."

"They watching us," Camp said, looking at the garage floor in thought. "How the hell did they know where Cooley was unless they followed him like we did? Either they watching Cooley or they watching us."

"That makes sense, but if they knew Cooley was at the church, why torch the house?" Kia asked. "Two different people?"

"Could be, but . . ."

"What are you thinkin'?"

"The more I think about the fire, the more it seemed half-hearted. It was a couple of shots to the front windows and the door, but that was it."

"Yeah, we know a little about that," Kai said with a smirk. "You hit the rooms people are likely to be in for that time of day, the bedrooms. And where was the patrol at the front of the house?"

"They had been switching off every three hours or so. They weren't there all the time," Camp explained.

"Doesn't matter. That's the way the police and prosecutor will spin it. Have you heard from your people in blue?"

"No, and I've been calling them."

That was it. Camp went to sleep, and Kai made some late-night phone calls of her own.

## Chapter Twenty-four

On Friday morning, their names were all over the papers, and the police were looking for them in relation to last night's shooting and firebombing. Even the damn president had nothing better to do than to tweet about the shooting, calling for a cancellation of the classic.

It would not be long before the Central American suppliers and financiers that ultimately ran Camp's business would be calling, getting anxious and losing patience. Little to no product was moving. Police were rounding up Camp's street soldiers all over town and holding them, all to apply pressure.

Sitting there doing nothing felt like death. This place would not stay hidden for long. The deed to Camp's safe house was in the name of a bogus corporation owned by another bogus corporation owned by a South American equity firm. Even with all that cover, eventually, some nosy Fox News-watching country-road dog walker would spot one of them or their cars and put two and two together.

All this time, Kai wondered what Camp and Cooley's wife were talking about in the spare bedroom. He had taken her breakfast about thirty minutes ago, and he was still in there. Kai was cleaning up the kitchen and watching the kid, who was singing along to some cartoon on cable television.

Anousha was awake when Camp bought in a tray of breakfast, egg-white Denver omelet, honeydew melon slices, wheat toast with Irish butter, and fresh-ground Ethiopian coffee. She sat in the middle of the queen-size bed with white wicker headboard and light-blue comforter. She was still in her clothes from yesterday. Camp felt his heart skip when he looked at her, despite the fact that she had the expression of a panicked, cornered animal.

"Camp, where is my baby?" she said, her voice strong despite the emotional warble in the back of her throat.

"She's fine; I made you breakfast. I—" he started to say as he lay the tray on the bed. Anousha leaped from her sitting position, grabbed the fork, and held it against Camp's throat.

"Muthafucka, I asked you where she was!?" she said, all hate and fear. She wrapped her other arm around the back of his neck. Her face was inches from his, and the fork moved ominously with the movement of his Adam's apple when he swallowed.

Camp stayed perfectly still save for his hands, which went up over his head.

"Mama, you're up!" Daria's voice broke the tension as the toddler bounded into the room. She jumped on the bed and immediately began eating a slice of melon. The two adults were still in mid-clinch, wondering about how this looked to the child. Daria finally paid closer attention to the adults.

"OOOOO – Mama," Daria said accusingly. "You not supposed to play with forks and knives!"

Anousha dropped the fork and dived on top of Daria, holding her tight and kissing her face.

"I told you she was fine," Camp said solemnly. "We were just getting acquainted."

Anousha pulled Daria back and started checking her little body. Daria complained about being kept from eating the rest of her mother's breakfast.

"Anousha, I wouldn't do that or anything to hurt either of you; I just want to talk."

"Yeah, right, I know what you want; why else would you bring us out here?"

"Do you know where you are?"

"Of course I know where I'm at . . ."

"How do you know, Mama? Do you know MB? Is he a friend of yours?" Daria asked.

"Daria, grown folks are talking. Now, hush," Anousha snapped.

"I promise I just want to talk; then you can go," Camp said. "CK can watch Daria."

"I like Mr. Davis, Mama; he can do coin tricks," Daria declared.

"Mr. Davis?" Anousha said, momentarily confused about whom Daria was referring to. Then she realized. "Oh, Daria, Mr. Davis. That's not a ma . . ."

"Not a what?" Daria asked.

Camp and even Anousha had to chuckle at the child's innocent gaffe. After a few seconds, Anousha relented and sent Daria back into the other room. Camp followed Daria to the bedroom door and called for Kai to come and get the child. As Kai came to take the child's hand, she made eye contact with Anousha.

"Hey," Kai said. Anousha waved with one hand but covered a slight grin with the other. Camp grinned as well.

"What?" Kai asked as she led Daria out of the room. "Don't know what you all laughing at . . ."

Camp closed the door, and then they were alone.

"So, you were trying to kill him?" Anousha said. "That's why you torched my house?"

"I didn't do that. Why would I do that with you and Daria in the house?"

"Don't bring her into this. You don't even know her."

"Yeah, why is that? I knew you for almost a year, or I thought I did."

"So, you just happen to be on my street just as it was being bombed?" she asked sarcastically.

"Nousha," he said, using the shortened nickname he'd devised back when they'd been lovers. "Why would I be torching your house if I'm also at the house across from the church shooting priests and old ladies, trying to off Cooley?"

"What?" she asked.

Then Camp just remembered she hadn't heard.

He left the room and returned with one of his tablets. He tapped on the screen. Then he let her read the story. She jumped from the bed, looking for her phone.

"Oh my God! I got to get to David. He is probably crazy with worry about us."

"David is fine. He's under police protection. You are fine here with us," Camp explained calmly

"We are not fine, Camp! People died at that church. That priest may die. Why was he even at a church?" Anousha thought aloud.

She was starting to hyperventilate.

"Where is my phone?"

"I would imagine burned up in the house."

"I have to call my parents. This is killing them."

"Not before we talk," Camp said.

"Fuck you, Camp. You can't hold us against our will. I got to find David."

"I'm not holding you against your will, and David is fine. He is in protective custody," he said, holding her arms.

She shrugged out of his hands.

"Just listen to me for one minute," he said.

She looked at him like a caged animal again.

"I can't be firebombing your house and shooting at your husband at the same time."

She pointed at the door.

"Yes, I could be at one location and CK at the other one, but I knew your husband was at the church. We followed him there. Why would we then firebomb your house?"

That was a point. She didn't have an answer for that one, but she wouldn't be put off that easy.

"And how do you know where the shots came from at the church? I know how," she replied, pointing at the door again. "Because your Japanese assassin was up there. To kill David. Now, call me a liar."

"She never fired a shot," Camp replied.

"Humph," she said.

"If CK was doing the shooting, there would not have been all that splatter, the priest, the old lady."

Anousha didn't answer. Camp kept going. "No, she would have been patient and waited as long as it took, and as soon as Cooley separated himself from the crowd—"

"Stop! Just stop, Camp!" Anousha screamed.

"And why am I trying to justify myself to your lying ass? He killed Butta in cold blood. Accident or not, the end is the same."

"So, why you got her doing your dirty work?" Anousha asked, and then she snapped her finger as if remembering something important. "You were waiting near my house in case CK didn't get the shot. You were going to do it yourself."

Camp just stared at her, his eyes dark and deadly.

You can't do it now," she said, her voice growing slightly hysterical. "I will tell everyone I know. That you brought me up here to shut me up. You'll have to kill all of us."

"No, I won't, but I will tell the world how you know me," Camp finally said in a voice cold as fresh freon.

"Hah, do you think I would care about that after you killed my husband?"

"Maybe, maybe not, but what about them bourgie, well-connected parents of yours, and what about Daria's classmates? Like I said before – nobody here is going to hurt you. But you start telling stories out of school and making threats? Then we will tell ALL the stories."

They were quiet for almost five minutes, each in their own thoughts. Angry, confused tears fell from Anousha's face, and it was all Camp could do not to go to her.

"Camp, this is a big fucking mess. My husband accidentally shoots my gangster ex-lover's cousin."

"Yeah, imagine my surprise when I found that out."

"I am asking you . . . no, begging you not to kill my husband or have him killed."

"In the meantime, Butta is dead, and his mother is a churchgoing, empty-prayer, zombie of a woman. Her baby is dead, and her life is a wreck because your husband made a mistake."

"I'm sorry," Anousha said solemnly. "In all this, I never said that to you. I know you and Butta were close. When I heard the news, when David told me what happened, I swear my heart broke for you."

"You know he was out of the business," Camp said. "And he did it himself. Just came to me one day and said he wasn't slanging no more."

"That's wonderful," Anousha said. "I saw the YouTube videos of his performances. He was amazing."

"It ain't right what they are writing about him, about him still being in the streets doing dirt. That wasn't him no more."

Camp allowed one tear to fall from his eye in front of someone other than Kai. Anousha never felt so conflicted in her life.

"I have a question for you. I have to know," he said. "What were we? I mean, I thought I knew, but now . . ."

"We were. . ." she said, and then she thought for a second or two, rolling her beautiful teary brown eyes to the ceiling. "We were a dangerously irresistible elixir that we both needed. We were medication, a salve for each other, but if you keep using medication past its purpose, you become . . ."

"Addicted," Camp finished. "What, were you medicating?"

She thought for several seconds, trying to gather her thoughts through the haze of everything that was happening. She needed to remember a time that seemed long ago but was less than fifteen months in the past.

"A lack of identity," she said. "Until you came along, there wasn't a period or an event in my life that was not scripted, planned, or monitored and then executed and evaluated. After all that 'good girl' plodding, I wasn't happy. I had a job, a husband, and even a baby, but I was just sliding through life from day to day. You were everything my life was not, spontaneous, non-affiliated in any way, and truly self-made."

"I thought you just wanted to run with a bad boy for a minute," Camp said, recalling his thoughts.

"There was something to that. The notorious, mysterious Camp Butterfield stepping to me at the Sky Lounge happy hour. You didn't know me or my people. You didn't talk to me because we grew up in Jack and Jill or because your father wanted some alliance with my father. You just saw me."

"And you got well; you got healed?" he asked.

"You help me find myself, what I liked, what I wanted, and how to love in my way and on my own terms," she said, looking at him.

"I think I may have stayed too long," Camp said. "I missed you, and I don't miss anybody."

"That's not addiction," she said. "I missed you too. I was forever changed by you. You were the same. CK told me that I was the only person you associated with that was not a criminal. You needed to change your compass of normal. It's part of your future. I like to think it's why you have been so successful for so long and still alive."

"I missed normal," he said, "having whole evenings where I didn't talk about product, marks, enemies, and the damn Colombians. I escaped inside you."

"But you didn't come after me," she said.

"And thank God I didn't," he said, chuckling. "I figured you were tired of walking on the wild side and decided to go back north of I-285. I never figured a husband and a kid."

"But you missed it?" she asked, her voice thick with emotion and innocence.

"Every day, even now. But you know you're not about that life. If you didn't wanna be down then . . . you know."

"Yeah, I know, but you missed it," she said again, the same way and from only inches away from him now.

She smelled like smoke, some latent perfume, and her natural scent, which he remembered lingering in his bed the entire day after she would leave.

There was a knock on the door. Then it opened. It was Kai.

"Camp, you got a call," she said, looking at the two of them close together.

Camp asked Anousha to stay in her room.

Once he got out into the hallway, he asked Kai to make Anousha a fresh breakfast and send her daughter in to her.

"I know I didn't see what I thought I saw," Kai said to him under her breath.

He waved her off and took the phone. It was the police on his payroll.

What's going on, boss?" one said. It was the kiss-ass.

"What the hell is going on out there?" Camp asked. "I pay you muthafuckas to be my ears on the street, and I can't find you."

"Hey, we were out there beating the bushes last night. It ain't easy after that mess you made at the church and the Cooley house."

"That wasn't me or CK," he said louder than he meant to.

"It wasn't?" the other one said. "Well, that explains a lot."

"What do you mean?"

"The mess, man; I know CK is a better shot than that. Everybody at Police Annex believes it's you. I assume you're at your hidey-hole in Rome?"

"You guessed right," Camp said, thankful for the subterfuge. The scrambler phone had an extra feature that sent its signal directly to an international satellite and pinged an artificial signal in Rome, GA. It made him appear a hundred miles north of where he actually was. "What happened to the patrol?" he asked.

"They are trying to figure that out; the patrol got the call over communicator to leave. The replacement was on the way. Then they found out Cooley had slipped out from under their noses. I guess he got a case of religion, huh?" one said with a chuckle.

"Not funny," Camp said.

"Hey, boss, it's obvious this was some vigilante group. The mess, and on top of that, they missed Cooley and killed a woman. We will keep our ears and eyes open and beat a few bushes. If we can steer this away from you, we will."

"Yeah, probably some of those black revolutionary clowns; they're tailor-made for it without much effort, and you'll be in the clear," the other one said.

"I'm in the clear because I didn't do it!" Camp shouted. He really didn't like these two, but they served their purpose.

"Right, right, boss, we understand," one of them said, his voice warm with assurance.

"Look, do you know where they are keeping Cooley?"

"Not yet, but we will find out soon enough," the other one said quickly.

"What about the other cops that were with him that night he killed my cousin?"

"No word whatsoever; it was a group of substitutes. All of them were from different precincts."

"Well, be careful beating the bushes; this whole thing is getting messy," Camp said.

They assured him they were being careful. Then the conversation stalled. There was something else they needed to say.

"Uh . . . boss, do you know an ex-cop from St. Louis named Phillips, goes by Lemon Boy?"

"I don't know anybody from St. Louis. Why?"

"Well, it's like this. The ex-cop Phillips is now doing security for that rapper MC TruLuv . . ."

"I've heard of TruLuv. What does this have to do with me?"

"It's about Butta. We were sitting in on a briefing between

our captain and the brass from the CNN/Centennial Park precinct. This guy Phillips and his team figured out where Butta was going that night."

"Where?"

"To see his baby mama."

"What? Nigga, Butta didn't have no kids!"

"Seems he was going to in about six or seven months."

"By who? What's her name?" Camp asked skeptically.

"Brianna Daniels," one of them said, and he gave her address.

Camp thought about the address and where Butta had been shot. He yelled for Kai, who was in the kitchen. He repeated the address to her, and she put it into the GPS app of her phone. When the map came up on the screen, she froze for a second and held it up for Camp to see. The girl lived straight north of where Butta had been shot and in the direction he'd been headed. Camp thought for a second or two and then turned his attention back to the phone.

"This Brianna? Is she some kin to . . .?"

"Yep," the other one said. "I looked into it. She's one of his nieces. That meat sandwich Butta was carrying was for her. It's her favorite."

That part of Atlanta was run by a well-known gambler named Dancing Disciple Daniels. He ran a small church in Midtown, on Argonne and Eighth Street, a building that would hold no more than seven hundred people. However, he had a congregation of over three thousand.

Instead of building a large megachurch, Dancing Disciple Daniels did his holy dance during each sermon by broadcasting via closed circuit from various banquet halls and civic centers. The church paid very well and the venue owners asked no questions. It was also well known that Disciple Daniels was into illegal gambling on a large scale, but between the lucrative rents he paid and the protection provided by the Russian mob moving into that part of Atlanta, he lived this duality with no interference.

Even though Daniels wasn't in the drug business, Camp always gave Disciple Daniels a wide berth. He was one of those old-school black gangsters who'd been able to stay alive and thrive for generations while younger, dumber competition had faded away. He and the Russians made a formidable enemy.

"Boss, what do you wanna do about this?" one asked.

"Nothing," Camp said flatly. He needed to process this information.

"Does Daniels know about the baby?" Camp asked.

"Don't think so," one said. "Phillips said the girl was keeping it a secret, like Butta."

Camp told them to keep this quiet. It would come out soon enough, but he needed time to think.

## Chapter Twenty-five

When the twins woke to the news of the president's tweet, they were full of protesting rage. Their three friends went down to the nearest drugstore and bought markers and construction boards to make new signs. They were practically rowdy when they left. The operatives had fresh orders to watch them closely and to contact the police and me if they saw our redneck friends from last night.

Teri and her operatives escorted a reluctant TruLuv to rehearsal for the Battle of the Bands that night. He wanted to do all kinds of ill-timed things. He wanted to go see Brianna, and he still wanted to reach out to Camp. In the end, he took his ass to the ATL Dome.

Then Bobby Sr. and I went to see Captain Sayles.

I covered the run-in with our redneck company from the previous night. He was more amused than irritated, thankful it hadn't resulted in more work for him or his staff. However, the smile fell off when we shared our news about Brianna and Butta.

"Wait a minute," he said and busily banged out a query on his worn keyboard. Then he called someone on the phone, asking them to come in immediately.

Bobby Sr. and I looked at each other, wondering what Pandora's Box we had kicked open. After about a minute of small talk, a female detective knocked on the door and entered the office. The only way I knew she was on the force was by the shield hanging from her wide white Gucci belt with gold buckle. Everything else about her screamed HBU freshman.

"This is Detective Howard," Captain Sayles said. We shook hands and introduced ourselves. She was polite and grown, which didn't jive with the visuals. She was just five foot five, with caramel-brown skin and shoulder-length, twisty curl extensions, and was about 130 pounds. She was in snug black jeans, white t-shirt with Burberry bottom trim, and a denim jacket. She had a pair of translucent J. Lo shades set on her head, half hidden in her teased hair.

"I guess by your stares that my cover is good," she said. "For what it's worth, I'm twenty-eight. Been a detective two years."

Bobby Sr. and I just nodded, smiled, and continued to stare. She had an athletic swagger and build.

"Detective, these gentlemen have news that you will find interesting."

As we gave her our information about the baby and how we'd come about it, Detective Howard's countenance went from pleasant to downright hostile.

"This is so fucked up," she said. "Who all knows?"

"Just my crew so far and maybe a hospital duty nurse," I explained.

"Is she there under her real name," she asked. She got her answer from the incredulous look on my face.

She rubbed the back of her neck, clearly pissed.

"So, how bad is this development?" Captain Sayles asked. "I want Lem and Bobby to hear your thoughts. They seem to be plugged into things out there, sharing their intel with the department."

"Yeah, well," she said, "they found out something I hadn't been able to glean though I've been practically living amongst these assholes."

"If it helps," I said, sensing the detective's hurt pride, "it was our female partner who found it first."

"No, it doesn't help," she said, thinking on that. "But I might like to meet her."

She pulled her phone from her back pocket and opened an app.

"Ok, here she is. For the past year, I have been posting up in the world of Leo C. Daniels, aka Dancing Disciple Daniels, a self-ordained minister of the New World Church of Progressive Christianity. Disciple Daniels has a congregation of over three thousand and a church that only holds seven hundred. He handles the overflow through broadcast locations all over town."

She paused for dramatic effect. I played along since we seemed to have stumbled into her briar patch.

"What's wrong with that?" I asked.

"Nothing," she said. "Until you start running illegal gambling in those same broadcast locations, banquet halls, lodge facilities, and union halls. Disciple Daniels was small time for years, operating out of private houses, dive bars, and in the back of the occasional dry cleaner. But in the last eighteen months, he has grown threefold. He has backers. We believe its Russian drug money."

"The Reve . . . uh, Disciple is pushing drugs?" I asked.

"No, at least not from what we can tell," Detective Howard said, consulting her digital notes. "The Russians usually like to handle the drug part themselves. Daniels is a black gangster from the very old school, preferring to stay in the crimes of sin, gambling, prostitution, and, from time to time, stolen goods."

Detective Howard tapped a few more times on her phone and continued. "The lady in question, Brianna Daniels, is his niece. She is from the innocent side of the family. Her mother is the Disciple's half-sister, same daddy but different mama. While the family all prayed together, they did not play together. Ms. Brianna is studious, halfway to a bachelor's degree in television communications. I guess that's why all the homecoming rigmarole."

"What's the history between Daniels and Camp Butterfield? They ever butt heads?" I asked.

"No, Camp is mostly I-20 south and mostly drugs and some grand theft auto, chopping cars. They are not in the same business as of yet."

"The Russians," I said.

"Exactly. We know they are making a big push to add territory in Atlanta. If they want to take Disciple Daniels south of I-20, there could be trouble. The fact that their beautiful pageant queen of a niece has been sullied by Camp

Butterfield's thug-ass kinfolk could be one of the things that tips the scale to war."

"Is Daniels that old school?" I asked.

"Not really, but that won't stop him from using it as a rallying cry for his street soldiers. And especially if the Russians want it that way," she explained. "I got to do some more digging into this. I need to know who in both families knows."

"Brianna and her mother on the Daniels side. I'm going to assume no one on the Butterfield side. Shawn was sneaking home to see her and not even telling his mother."

"He is . . . was good at that. I got no indication. Mind you, that was the non-criminal side of the family and not my main focus."

"Nobody's blaming you for anything, Detective," Captain Sayles said. "I wanted to bring you in to share information going both ways."

"So, what's your next move, Phillips?" Detective Howard asked, her voice still containing remnants of sarcasm.

"Nothing," I assured her. "I was on the force in St. Louis; I have no law enforcement fantasies."

"Good," she said, pocketing her phone and walking for the door. "Because this could get as nasty as boiled Brussel sprouts."

***

Madina decided to see how the Battle of the Bands rehearsals were going. She had to take a break from all of those meetings and conference calls.

For all practical purposes, the Big Boo Classic was a success. The sold-out step show had actually pinged on Nielsen polls, peaking higher than *Real Housewives* and just behind the top-rated scripted Friday night police show.

The police shooting of poor Shawn Butterfield was sparking out of control. The shooting at the church and firebombing was putting a damper on things. She had tried to pay tribute to the kid in some way, but it had tied her classic to violence in the city. Advertisers were asking for assurances. HBU officials, who were already skeptical of a new classic, were grumbling. She was at the pivotal part of this huge project. It could go big or go bad if she didn't watch it, and that could hurt KeeVon's future as well as her own.

She walked past a large wood-floored rehearsal salon. About a hundred feet square, it was used by the teams to walk through play schemes and by cheerleaders to choreograph their routines. While the rest of the band was on the field, the drum majors were working through their routines in this room. The Birmingham A&M majors were in the salon now. She watched for a few minutes, enjoying the dynamic, confident body movements of the three men of the Marching Pride.

*Three men?* she thought. *Where is what's her name?*

She walked into the room and approached one of the students watching the drum major rehearsal.

"Where's the girl drum major?" she asked as if trying to remember her name.

"You mean Gina P?" the student asked. Madina nodded.

He was short, about five feet seven inches, glasses, dark complexion, and a head covered in wooly, pillowy black hair. He reminded Madina of a younger version of Posdnous – Plug One from De La Soul.

"She wasn't feeling good, so Dr. Tolliver had her sit out and worked a kid in from the drum line who had some skills."

"Where is she?" Madina asked.

"In the break room with the red sofas," Baby Pos said, pointing in the right direction.

She found Gina Pombo where the boy had said she would be. She was still in her rehearsal workout clothes. Something didn't smell right with this. The girl Madina had met in the executive offices a couple of days ago did not seem to be the type that would let a stomachache or some monthly cramps get the best of her.

"Hey, Ms. Pombo, how you doing?" Madina asked as she walked into the break room.

Gino looked up from her phone. She appeared to be watching videos of past performances. "Hey, I'm good," she said. She sounded like a totally different person, preoccupied and defeated.

"They say you not feeling like rehearsal? Gotta be pretty bad to bow out on the day of the show," Madina said, trying to evoke some bedside manner, not her strong suit.

"Yeah, I'm not sure," Gina said, avoiding eye contact.

"Not sure about what? Your ability?"

"NO, I'm good on my skills," she said, showing a bit of that old fire. "Is that what they said out there?"

"Gina, I'm only interested in what you got to tell me," Madina said. "You know you stepping into some important shoes. Shawn seemed like a hell of a drum major."

"He was."

"Were you two friends?"

Silence as the tears started to well up in Gina's eyes.

"Well, don't you want to do justice to your friend's memory?"

Nods and now tears.

"Then we can't let him down or show weakness to those boys out there."

That was when it all came out. Gino talked non-stop for five minutes about the intimidation, the malicious sexual touching. She talked about how she hadn't been eating or sleeping and had started taking pills to help with both. She had lost weight, and her hair was falling out.

"Why did you not tell anyone?" Madina asked, barely able to stop herself from marching into that rehearsal in a rage and killing that boy.

"You know how it is, Ms. Sherman. It's a thin line between reporting and being a whiny, complaining woman. He's a senior, so I figured once he was gone, I would still have one or two more years to perform."

As Madina walked back down to the rehearsal hall, her thoughts oscillated back and forth. On one hand, she had to stay focused on the big picture, big decisions, and her son's brand. On the other, she was a woman of influence who had just been told about a straight-up sexual harassment incident that she could fix.

*How do I do this without washing away one more black man?* she thought despite her rage. These were still very young people.

She found Dr. Tolliver in the rehearsal hall when she returned. He was standing next to MC TruLuv, the rapper who was scheduled to perform with both bands at the battle and during halftime at the game. She remembered that TruLuv was one of the new wave of artists like Chance the Rapper or Lupe Fiasco, and she had an idea.

"That's a major accusation; you got any proof?" Dr. Tolliver said expectantly after Madina explained what Gina Pombo had told her. She understood the director had a duty to protect his students even from each other. "I have never heard anything like this about MC. Gina has never said anything to me in the past."

"What would you have done if she had?" Madina asked.

"I would have investigated it," Dr. Tolliver answered.

"How? How do you investigate these?" TruLuv asked with sincere interest.

"Well, it would take time . . ." Dr. Tolliver said. He was

perspiring now, realizing this was not just a spat between students.

"Good. While you slowly drag your ass around an investigation, your boy can watch from the stands," she said.

"Wait! We got a battle in eight hours. He's our best drum major."

"I will not put a known molester of women on my field," she said.

"Your field?"

"Yes, my field, Dr. Tolliver. I set this classic up, made the connection between the schools, the conferences, the dome, and the networks. So, yes," she said, ending with two hard slaps to her own chest. "MY field."

"I'll have to take this up with my president," he said haughtily.

"Please do," Madina said with a laugh. "Let's see, you got, on one hand, one of the biggest paydays for any HBU school, and on the other hand, we got one little asshole you're trying to protect. Go ahead, Dr. Tolliver, and you can be sitting in the stands next to him.

"I'll pull my band," Dr. Tolliver responded.

"Fine, I'm sure Banneker College can fill your time. Either way, that little fucker doesn't see the field."

"But in that case, unfortunately, neither would Ms. Pombo," TruLuv said, interjecting into this shouting match.

"TruLuv, you gotta stand up for this girl," Madina implored.

"I do stand up for her; I'm sure her director does as well. Right, Dr. Tolliver?"

"Of . . . of course I do. I wouldn't have given her this opportunity if I didn't believe in her."

"You mean given her the opportunity she earned?" Madina snapped back.

"Yes, that's what I said." Dr. Tolliver mumbled.

"Good," said TruLuv. "So, I think we should all do everything we can to get our drum major on the field. Ms. Madina, can you manage to get her ready for rehearsal? Tell her it's a polite request from me."

Madina nodded that she could.

"Next, Dr. Tolliver can you move Mr. Clark out to the band on the field?"

"But when is he supposed to rehearse?"

"If he is as good as you say, he should be fine," TruLuv said. "We need to keep them apart until performance time."

"What difference does that make?" Madina said again. "He's not going to be in it."

"I am going to make some phone calls to see what I can find out; Dr. Tolliver, I advise you do the same. Investigate as best you can in this short period of time. Make discreet inquiries with the seniors in the band. Depending on what we find out, we can make a fair decision just before performance time," TruLuv explained, looking at the other two.

"I just don't like my day being hijacked by a student," Dr. Tolliver mumbled.

"Look at it this way," TruLuv explained as he tapped a number into his phone. "Ms. Pombo could have opened up to all her friends on Facebook instead of Ms. Madina. Think of how busy we all would be if she had done that."

***

Following TruLuv's request, Bobby Sr. and I found our way to the dome. The Battle of the Bands crowd was inside. Outside was the True America Concert, sponsored by the new president. The raucous concert of local country rock bands was being held on the grounds just outside the dome. The crowd was filled with a variety of characters, all white. I thought that was strange coming from a city with a more than its fair share of African-American and Latino country music fans.

There were some characters that looked like our friends from last night, but there were also some true music fans out for a night of music. Even Bobby Sr., an old-school Irish kid from South St. Louis, thought it looked weird. I thought about what would happen when the Battle of the Bands crowd let out at the end of the event. The Atlanta Police Department was out in full force. They were going to earn their money tonight.

Teri met us at one of the rear entrances. She had security wave us into an interior parking lot reserved for players during football season.

"How is our boy?" I asked, focusing on our main objective.

"He's good," Teri said, fully focused. "Found himself officiating a mess, but nothing that will get him killed."

"Good, because there's enough of that going on outside of these walls," I said.

We walked down a series of halls until we came to some offices. They were too small to be dressing rooms. TruLuv was there along with some heavy hitters from the Big Boo Classic: Madina Sherman, the executive organizer of the event, Dr. Tolliver, music director for Birmingham A&M, Charles Bullock, event director for the Dome, and a young man sitting in the corner with an angry expression. I assumed he was the reason behind all the heartburn.

"Thank you, everybody, for being here. I know we can get through this and get back to the show. Television cameras are rolling tonight," TruLuv explained. "Milton, we got an issue, and it involves you."

"I just want to say one thing," Milton Clark said. He made his eyes innocent and smiled like a dental model. "There has been some mistake. My only objective has always been to create a strong drum corps. I got a lot invested in it. As the leader, I have to be kind of tough sometimes."

"Being tough? Is that what you call it when you pin a woman against the wall and grope between her legs?" Madina said.

Milton Clark feigned surprise and hurt. He was good at it, but I'd seen enough of it to know that he was putting it on just a tad too much.

"Wait, we only have the girl's word on that," Dr. Tolliver said. "Milton explained that she had complained to him about the workout, the regimen, the sacrifices he commanded from his other drum majors to be great."

"Ms. Madina, TruLuv, the Marching Pride and the Roaring III have a rich tradition," said Milton, "We have won awards from Atlanta to Tokyo. As the senior member, I can't let the quality fall. But I assure you that I never used tactics like this. I got three sisters and a mama. They taught me to respect women."

"I asked the other drum majors and some of the band members, and they said they had seen no evidence of what Gina Pombo was talking about," Dr. Tolliver said. "What did you find, Madina?"

"I'm trying to run a damn classic, so I didn't have a chance to investigate. I got a smart, talented, accomplished young lady who has been driven off her calling by one of her brothers in the drum majors, the leader of the group. TruLuv, my vote is the same. Mr. Clark needs to find a seat in the stands."

There were guffaws and gasps among the group, especially from Milton.

"Madina, the kid is a well-known asset on the field. We got a lot of boosters and alumni in the stands," Charles said. "They want to see Milton in the group. They will ask why he's not out there."

"We'll say he's sick or hurt," Madina replied dismissively. "I got two dynamic bands AND two badass drum corps. That will sell on television. That will get me that Nielsen ping and excite the advertisers. Mr. Clark's absence only affects which of the bands wins. I personally don't care which one wins."

"Without me, you might as well hand the trophy to Banneker," Milton said, and there it was. The church boy innocence was gone, and the slick, world-savvy ladies' man of the Roaring III was there.

I moved closer to TruLuv to give him what he had asked for, but he gave me a look that said, *No, no, not yet.*

Then MC TruLuv, my son, did something that I can only describe as some "cool shit." He walked over to Milton and stood right in front of him.

"Man, one chance. You tell the absolute truth about you and Gina, and no matter how bad it is, you will get my vote tonight."

The whole room was thrown off by this. I could hear Madina mumbling under her breath.

The room was quiet for almost a minute. TruLuv never said another word. Only Bobby Sr. and I knew the game he was playing, and it took everything to keep from grinning with pride.

"I promise you, TruLuv. I ain't do none of that stuff," Milton said, sitting back in his chair, feeling a sense of relief he should not have felt. TruLuv stared at him for several seconds, his expression truly sad, like he'd found his favorite pet dead in the street.

"Ok, Lem, I'm ready for what you found," he said with a sigh. He walked to the other side of the room and stood next to Madina.

I pulled my phone out and opened the Notes application.

"Milton M. Clark, aka MC, aka ShadyMil. Arrested in 2013, University of Southwest New Mexico, sexual assault. Charges dropped from lack of evidence. Arrested 2015, Savannah, Georgia, domestic violence. Charges reduced. Arrested 2015, Bessemer, Alabama, sexual assault. Charges dropped when victim refused to press charges. Person of interest 2016, Atlanta, Georgia, present during a possible gang rape. Case pending but never closed."

"Wait, who is this guy? Where did he get this?" Dr. Tolliver said.

"It's all public record," I said. "If you had really tried to look."

"This is my security detail," TruLuv said. "I had them do some simple checking through public records."

"Hey, man, them girls was crazy," Milton said. "You see I ain't never do no time."

"But there are twenty different 'crazy' girls on this list," I said.

"Twenty?" Madina said.

TruLuv motioned for her to hold her thought. "Lem, did you do that other thing?" he asked.

"Most definitely," I said. "My partner and I met with Brianna Daniels."

"He fucked with my classic queen?" Madina asked.

"No. Ms. Daniels, we have found out, was Butta's girlfriend. We asked if Butta had ever shared stories about Ms. Pombo and Milton. It turns out he had," I explained as I scrolled through my phone.

"It took her a while to find it; turns out she kept ALL his texts."

When I found what she had shared with me, I handed the phone to TruLuv, who read it aloud.

> *Brianna: How was practice?*
>
> *Butta: Good, can't wait for the band competitions. We should crush this year.*
>
> *Brianna: Cocky ass.*
>
> *Butta: Just confident! BTW – we got a nice secret weapon.*
>
> *Brianna: ??*
>
> *Butta: A female drum major. She's good.*
>
> *Brianna: Really?*
>
> *Butta: Real Talk. She's tough. I'm proud of her. She gives us something we don't have.*
>
> *Brianna: That's cool; just don't get too proud Papa.*
>
> *Butta: LOLOL. Never. As hard as I had to work to get a first date with you. Sheeeeet*
>
> *Brianna: Right answer.*
>
> *Butta: Can't say the same for Milt. He been pushing up on her.*
>
> *Brianna: Tryin' to holla at her.*
>
> *Butta: Naw, like riding her, giving her a hard time.*

*Brianna: Hazing.*

*Butta: This is more. It's like personal with him. I've heard him complaining about her with Jesse and some of the seniors.*

*Brianna: Because she's a she.*

*Butta: I think so. But I been keeping an eye out for her. I think she makes us stronger.*

*Brianna: My man the protector.*

Madina pulled her portable communicator walkie-talkie from her hip and requested security report to her location immediately. Then, stepping into the middle of the room, she took control of her event.

"Dr. Tolliver, first, you got one hour to get your band ready to roll with Gina Pombo front and center, paying proper tribute to Shawn Butterfield. Second, you will get Mr. Clark out of that goddamn uniform and removed from this facility. If you don't, my security will have him removed. Third, after this weekend, I will do everything in my power to convince Gina Pombo to file charges, and I guarantee you this time, it will go to trial."

Dr. Tolliver motioned for Milton to follow him out of the room. Madina looked at Charles, who just waved his hand and left the room. Then she turned to us.

"What's your name?" she asked me. I introduced myself and the rest of the team.

"That's was some pretty quick work," she said with a smile. "It takes all of you to protect TruLuv? Because I could use some help on game day."

"He can be a handful," I said playfully. "But we will be around. If we hear anything or see anything, we got your back."

"Yeah, I could use some checking on my back by the right person," Madina said with a playful glance at her curvy hips.

"Madina, dang!" TruLuv said. "C'mon, Pop, I got to get in position. The show's about to start."

I stood there, not knowing which surprised me more, the flirt from the no-nonsense power broker or TruLuv calling me Pop.

## Chapter Twenty-six

The Battle of the Bands was an amazing event. Like the step show the day before, it had announcers and commentators describing every facet of the show. They had fitted leaders of every section with microphones, which would allow them to bring high-quality audio from the field to the television audience. They were also using picture-in-picture slow-motion replay so they could isolate and show all the artistry, athleticism, and agility of the drum majors and the dancers.

I stood in the tunnel where the bands came out. Banneker College was first. They started deep in the back of the tunnel, about thirty feet from the opening.

**"Ladies and gentlemen, feel the shake, feel the rumble! When they growl, the others stumble! Make some noise for the Marching Bruins of Banneker College!"**

Before the announcer could end his introduction, the Banneker Bruins were yelling like crazed warriors going into battle. They were in all-white uniforms with Bear Claw markings surrounding large rustic B's on the front and back. They took the field like they were going to war, every face painted with some kind of festive coloring like tribal Indians. The base drummers banged their charges in rhythmic unison like the steps of a giant bear upon the earth.

Following them at a casual stroll was Dr. Brazille, the music director. A light-skinned black man from New Orleans, he wore white slacks and shoes, a Bruins-brown sports coat, and matching brown shirt and white tie. His Creole hair was part of the performance. Like now, it always started in a combed-back, slicked-down style. By the end of the performance, it would be in a curly frenzy all over his sweat-and-blood-infused face, a la Cab Calloway.

The Bruins started with "Don't Stop 'Til You Get Enough" by Michael Jackson, "Wild Thoughts" by DJ Khalid and Rhianna, and "Single Ladies" by Beyoncé.

The Claw Crew – Banneker's drum majors – were three men, all tall and heavy, resembling actual bears. However, they moved with the agility of Broadway tap dancers. They rolled their middles and popped and locked to the beat like they were straight out of a hip hop video.

The head drum major, wearing a cape with the letters PB on it, for Papa Bear, handled the flips and splits, which he did almost continuously. He did all this without losing his headpiece. Their performance ended when TruLuv took the field and rapped and sang to their version of his song "Speak Your Mind."

Local high school drum corps performed during intermission. They wowed the crowd, performing their own versions of the final scene from the motion picture *Drumline*.

Then it was time for the Birmingham A&M Marching Pride. Their uniforms were the same golden color of a lion's mane, with the blue, black, and orange jeweled face of a lion on the back. The headpieces were in the shape of a lion's head, with furry attachments to simulate the mane.

**"Ladies and gentlemen, this ain't no children's story with actors in the roles. This is the savannah, where the king of the cats patrols. And when they take the field, they won't be denied. Mothers, guard your children. It's the A&M Marching Pride!"**

They moved to the opening of the tunnel and lined up with military precision. Then the two drum majors moved out onto the field just in front of the tunnel. Gina Pombo was on the right.

I looked for nerves after everything she had been through in the last three days. She was shorter than the other drum major, but she was in the zone, showing the ferocity and intensity required of her position.

They counted off, and the Marching Pride took the field to "Jungle Love" by Morris Day and The Time. They separated into four separate two-person lines representing the lion's footprint as it moves across the proverbial African grasslands. Gina led two of the lines; the other drum major led the other two lines.

Both wore short capes. Gina's cape bore the letters SB on it.

Once in formation, they moved immediately into their songs, "Stand Up" by Ludacris and "Crazy In Love" by Beyoncé and Jay-Z.

Bobby Sr. rolled up next to me and handed me an iPad streaming the broadcast feed. The images were amazing as they moved from the overhead view to the field view, moving between the marching lines. The closeups of the drum majors made you feel like you were right next to them. Gina Pombo looked great. There is a difference between male and female drum majors. They both move with power and finesse, but the showmanship is slightly different. I wasn't sure if it was physical, mental, or both. I just knew Gina Pombo was a dynamo who could more than hold her own.

When it came to their last number, TruLuv retook the field to cheers and applause. There was an electric guitar slung over his shoulder. He stood in front of the Marching Pride, facing the crowd. Tech hands brought him a microphone and connected his guitar.

"Ladies and gentlemen, as you know, the Marching Pride recently lost a member of the drum major corps, Mr. Shawn Butterfield," TruLuv announced. The crowd applauded. "You all knew him as Shawn, but to us, he was Butta!"

The band sent up a cheer.

"Instead of one of my songs, I will accompany the band in a tribute to their fallen friend."

He extended the mic to the drum majors. After a second, Gina Pombo stepped forward. She took the mic from TruLuv, and you could clearly see her hand shaking and her shoulders heaving. TruLuv hugged her for several seconds, murmuring words of encouragement. Gina Pombo nodded several times to what he was saying, took a deep breath, wiped at her face to clear her emotions, and addressed the audience.

"Butta was not just my bandmate. He was my mentor, my protector, my brother, and my friend."

The crowd applauded.

"I am performing in his spot among the Marching Pride tonight, and I'm wearing his initials on my uniform. Tonight, we perform to an original arrangement by Shawn himself. This is called 'Butta's Beat.'"

The song was reminiscent of a New Orleans second line jam. The tubas and trombones took control of the beat and rhythm. Then the trumpets came and went with TruLuv's guitar riffs to create a second line dance jam interspersed with segments that could only be described as high jazz. The band played loud and strong. They moved with all the physical abandon that young folks have.

Halfway through the song, the drumline came forward and formed a semicircle around Gina Pombo. For the next two minutes, it was drums, trumpets, and guitar.

Gina performed a solo performance that was part dance, part acrobatic wonder. She high-stepped, kicked, flipped, spun, and split. All of this was done to a powerful groove that had the crowd moving in their seats and waving tissues, handkerchiefs, and lighted cell phones.

The television moved across the seats from one tearful face to the other. Dr. Tolliver stood at his platform, his eyes streaming with tearful emotion.

When she finished and the camera closed in on her face, it was wet from sweat, but her eyes were dry orbs of defiance and pride.

The audience stood and applauded for the entire minute, and she stayed in her final split. They were so loud the drumline leaders had to use hand signals to get the rest of the band into exit formation. The crowd continued to scream as they marched off while still playing "Butta's Beat." TruLuv stayed on the field and continued to accompany them.

On Hunnicutt Avenue, just south of Georgia Tech, Brianna Daniels sobbed from pride and a broken heart as she watched the broadcast. In his office in South Fulton County, Camp Butterfield watched the dedication with pride. He cried a single tear as he drank too much cognac. He fought against the blackness pushing to take over his soul.

There was magic in the dome that night. Emotion carried the place past the awarding of the trophy for the Battle of the Bands.

Bobby Sr. made his way to the exit, while I headed up to the offices on the second floor. Madina was in one of the executive offices, toasting with a bunch of important men who smelled like money. I gave her a wave, and she motioned for me to come in as she separated herself from the others.

"Ratings just came in," she said as she hugged me like a long-lost lover, her face right against mine. "We actually carried the last half-hour. We were the highest-rated show on network tonight."

"Great! Congratulations," I said, a little surprised, but pleasantly so. "Gina did a great job!"

"Yes, she did," Madina said, her eyes tearing from Gina's performance and the first stage of inebriation from Moet Champagne. "That girl is dynamite."

"Well, I got to get my people home," I said, but she held my arm.

"We got a problem outside," she started to explain.

## Chapter Twenty-seven

True to the president's word, the fairgrounds adjacent to the dome were being used for his True America Celebration. While the Big Boo Classic Battle of the Bands took place inside the dome, the fairgrounds outside the dome had filled up with a mostly Caucasian crowd listening to country music, muscle trucks, and a few ten-foot-tall Confederate flags.

Despite the success of the event tonight, Madina worried what would happen when the mostly African-American crowd was released from the dome and out to where the True American Celebration was taking place. I told her we would stick around to assist police once we got TruLuv off and away.

I reached the exit and peeked out the front doors of the dome. The True American Celebration was in full swing. The majority of it seemed like a typical country music concert. However, here and there were troubling elements: Confederate flags tall as buildings and signs that read "Speak English or Leave," "One America, One way," and "Make America Prosperous for Real Americans."

"Come in, Exit Patrol," I said into my communicator. "What's the status? Where you are?"

"It's a damn zoo out here," Bobby Sr. replied. "I'm moving from the rear parking lot adjacent to the fairgrounds, moving inside the stadium security gate."

"Remote Unit, where are you?"

"Remote Unit here. We have the packages and are moving through traffic to the home base. ETA ten minutes."

I sighed with relief. The operatives with Chunky and Choppy and their friends had moved out of the area before things had gotten crazy.

"Remote Unit, please report in once the packages are off the street."

"Teri, how is our package?" I asked Teri about TruLuv.

"He's finishing autographs now. We will be moving to transportation in five minutes," she answered.

"Limit his exposure; keep him from windows. There are dangerous potentials just outside the dome."

"Copy that," Teri said.

I moved back up to the exits, trying to make eye contact with Bobby Sr.'s vehicle. I ran into Captain Sayles.

"Phillips, I should have known you would be around here."

I asked how his officers were holding up.

"Just barely. There's too many exits, too many points for conflict to happen."

"I got five operatives here. How can I help the rest of the security?"

"The back halls," he said rapidly. "We're rerouting the Battle of the Bands audience out the south exit, away from the fairgrounds. They're grumbling about having to walk around the long way to their cars, but I don't care. We've already found about fifty attendees trying to go back the other way. I got men on the north doors, but your guys can guard the halls between the two exits and steer people the right way."

Twenty minutes later, we had TruLuv in one of the transports with Teri and her operatives, heading for home base. Bobby Sr. and I were in one of the main hall arteries that led to the exits. We'd kept two operatives with us. True to Captain Sayles's word, we turned about a hundred people back to the rear exit. They didn't like it and complained about heart conditions and bad knees. Madina had a few wheeled people movers dispatched to carry their attitudinal behinds back in the direction from which they'd come. There were a few young brave African-American men blustering that way. They had put two and two together, realizing we were avoiding possible bad interactions with the True American Concert crowd.

"Man, why we got to go around the long way; ain't nobody asking them white folks to go around the long way or move over," the loud one said.

"Young man, it's just about safety and people control. Letting you all out the front would just put too many people in too small a space," I explained.

He said I was full of it and that we were not the police. It was six of them and four of us, but their hearts weren't really in it. The operatives stepped forward, letting their jackets waft open to reveal their sidearms. While the young men were staring at that, Bobby Sr. expanded his iBOT wheelchair, putting him at about six feet. At some point, he pulled his collapsible baton, issued by the British police.

I made a request for police assistance at my position in my communicator, loud enough for them to hear. Right on time, a response squawked back.

"Gentlemen, you can go back, or you can go to jail, but you ain't going down this hallway," I said. Soon, we watched as they headed back, mumbling curses.

About thirty minutes later, we got the all-clear message from Captain Sayles and Madina Sherman's staff. As we walked to the opposite exit, we heard a noise from one of the bathrooms.

Bobby stayed in the extended position, but when I looked in his lap, he had swapped his baton for his Glock semi-automatic. I pulled my Beretta and held it in the down position. I ordered the operatives to stay outside the bathroom door.

"Don't let anyone out and come in only if I yell for you," I explained.

I knelt on one knee and pushed the door open as far as it would go. We waited one second, two seconds, three seconds. Bobby Sr. rolled in, gun drawn on his insistence. I came in behind him, crouched behind the chair. At first, there was no one to be seen. The bathroom was rectangular, with a bank of sinks and mirrors on the left and toilet stalls down the right. There were two urinals just behind the entry doors.

Bobby Sr. and I communicated with our hands. Once we got it together, he rolled to the door, opened it, and let it close as if he'd gone out. While he did that, I climbed up on the vanity between the sinks. I squatted on my haunches, my pistol resting next to me. I was positive there was someone in the bathroom. I suspected they would eventually step off the toilets and put feet down in one of the stalls. We would wait them out instead of searching the stalls and catching a spray of who knows what in the face.

Then we heard grunting and movement in the ceiling. One of the suspended two-by-four ceiling tiles lifted out of its track, followed by a curse.

"Ok, get your ass down here!" I yelled, jumping off the vanity. I moved to the far end of the bathroom. Bobby Sr. was still at the other end by the entry door. I didn't stay perfectly still. We were thinking the same thing: *What if our ceiling dwellers are armed?* If they decided to fire down on us, we would not see it coming.

I heard mumbling and cursing and more movement. This was ridiculous.

"Bobby, you got the rubber gun?" I asked.

"Of course," he said, rolling over and handing me a short-barrel rifle. I never understood where on those chairs he hid all that firepower.

I cocked it and sprayed the ceiling over the first toilet stall with rubber pellets. The force of the pellets went through the ceiling tiles and hit at least one of them. I know because he came falling through the ceiling. He bounced off the top of the stall wall, flipped outside the stalls, cracked his shoulder on the urinal, and landed face down on the bathroom floor. He jumped up and attempted to run from the bathroom, but he was detained by the operatives waiting outside.

We settled the fallen one on the floor in the hall outside the bathroom and called for police backup. While we waited, I kept watching the character who'd fallen from the ceiling. He looked familiar. We didn't question him. That was a police job. He couldn't go far anyway. The fall had sprained his ankle and dislocated his shoulder. A minute later, Atlanta Metro officers removed him, limping and all. Two additional officers followed and went into the ceiling cavity after any others.

Bobby Sr. and I drove home in exhausted silence. The operatives were sleeping in the back. We got home and checked the weapons. Bobby Jr. left a message for us to be heads-up tomorrow. He would check in early before the game.

I went to the bar and made a Booker's straight in one of the beautiful cut crystal glasses that had come with the rental house. It would send me straight to sleep.

Bobby Sr. was switching out charges on his chairs and clicking on that master keyboard of his, checking on his lures on the dark web discussion boards.

"It was a good night, huh?" TruLuv's voice said behind me.

He was in pajama pants and a t-shirt. He looked like a teenager. It was times like this, when he wasn't "on stage," that I tried to steal close looks to see resemblances.

"Yeah, that Gina Pombo had the house full of wet Kleenex," I said, chuckling behind my drink. "Good work on the axe."

"Listen to you, man," TruLuv said, "trying to use the industry slang. I get it. Thanks, though. It was pretty emotional. I had to breathe through my mouth to get through without tearing up past being able to see."

I nodded and sipped my drink.

"Hey, uh, you think I could have a pull of that Booker's?" TruLuv asked.

"Whaaaaa?" I said, truly surprised. "The holistic, clean-living TruLuv?"

"Yeah, yeah," he said, waving off my teasing. "I'm just wound up; I did my breathing and meditation and drank some lemon balm tea."

"Lemon balm tea?" I said, snickering. "Ok, ok, at least give me the privilege of making you a drink."

"Just a small one, Pop," he said. "I don't drink those kitchen-size drinks you make."

I laughed harder than the joke called for. He'd called me Pop again, and it was my turn to get soggy-eyed. I gave them a quick finger wipe while I made his very weak Booker's and water with a little syrup to take the edge off.

I returned to the sitting area. He was on the sofa, so I took the overstuffed chair adjacent to him. He sipped his drink and made a face, but he gave me a thumbs up. Thinking back on the day, I remembered something.

"I got a question. That scene with Milton Clark. offering him the out? How did you know it would go the way it did?"

"I thought all afternoon about the time I spent with the drum majors last summer. I got to know them as people. Gina Pombo was no shrinking violet, and she wasn't a person who used lies to achieve her ends."

"And you knew Milton was a scumbag?" I asked.

"No, but I remember him being very insecure. I remembered how Butta, Jesse, Gina, and the others had to be careful how they spoke to him, how they joked with him, lest he take it as a personal attack. I could see someone like that being threatened by a personality like Gina's. I also figured it wasn't the first time."

I nodded as I watched him over my drink. He took another sip, then a bigger sip, and then gulp it down until it was gone.

"Besides," he said as he stood, "I could tell by the look on your face when you walked in that my hunch was right."

"And yet you wanted to give him an out?" I said.

"Yeah, I did. Milton didn't get that way on his own. Despite his looks, he's just twenty-two years old. That's a few years younger than me. He was raised by a series of aunts and foster parents. Despite that, he's made his way to the top of the drum major heap."

"I see," I said.

"Don't get me wrong," he continued. "Part of me wants to put his ass under the ground for what he did to Gina and countless others, but then, how many people are lining up to do that to black men in this country. I don't know what the answer is, but it's somewhere in the middle."

He wished me goodnight, and I did the same, contemplating the complicated quandary he had left before me.

## Chapter Twenty-eight

Camp Butterfield woke up on Saturday feeling like crap. Watching the Battle of the Bands and the tribute to Butta had torn him up. He'd watched and recorded it alone in his bedroom. He had come out of his room two times to get another bottle of booze.

He'd wanted to call his contacts to find out where Cooley was and go out with a blast. Then he'd heard Daria laughing and giggling in the bedroom with her mother and joking with Kai. In his drunken stupor, he'd even fantasized about killing Cooley and taking his place in Anousha's life. His thoughts had been a mess.

By the end of the night, he'd told Kai to just take Anousha and Daria wherever they wanted to go. He didn't think she would go to the police, but he was past caring. He had bigger things brewing. The Colombians and the money from Belize were calling. Kai had been putting them off, but at some point, he had to talk to them to assure them. If he couldn't pull this off, it would be a matter of time before people smelled the cracks in his armor.

Butta was gone forever. Cooley probably wouldn't make it much longer. One of these vigilante groups would be successful at some point. Lying in bed, still wearing his clothes from yesterday, he just wanted to get Anousha to her parents' house.

In one of the other bedrooms, Anousha had called her parents last night, not giving her location or who she was with but requesting they call the police to let David know she and the baby were safe. They didn't like it, but that wouldn't be the last time Anousha would do something they didn't like. Besides, she wasn't leaving until she got the feeling that Camp wasn't going to come after her husband for good.

He'd said he hadn't been behind the attacks on her family, and she believed him. It was why she'd stayed. If there were others trying to kill them, she and Daria were in one of the safest places in the city, the last place anyone would think to look.

Lying in his stinking clothes and body odor, Camp thought he heard a soft knock on his door. He figured it was Kai checking on him. He was partially right.

"I'm up," he said groggily as he opened his door. Then he noticed Kai was dressed in ceremonial Japanese clothing. Women's clothing.

"Take your time and get dressed," she said solemnly. "We got company that will help us with our predicament."

"Who?" he asked.

Kai was solemn and serious. "You will see," she said. "Get dressed. I might suggest you choose a suit."

"What about Anousha and the baby?" Camp asked.

"They are in their bedrooms, out of sight of our guests," Kai said. Her calm was spooky. Was it the police? Was it the Colombians?

Camp quickly showered and shaved. He found his blue Hugo Boss suit. He came downstairs and slowly walked around to the living room.

"In the kitchen, Camp," Kai called out to him.

He reversed his direction, going through the dining room. He saw her standing straight, her hands folded in front of her. He continued until he could see the entire kitchen.

He barely registered everyone else in the room when his eyes landed on Disciple Daniels sitting on a bar stool at the kitchen counter. He was sipping from a coffee cup and staring at Camp with an amused expression. He looked at Camp as if he were a disheveled kid arriving late for school.

To keep from letting it bother him, he turned his attention to the others. Two of Daniels's soldiers were standing behind him, looking uncomfortable between the countertop and center island. Then there was a well-dressed Asian man sitting on a stool behind Kai. He was also sipping a light-brown liquid from a glass. It was too light to be bourbon or cognac, especially at this time of day. However, it didn't appear to be tea or coffee either.

"Camp, you know Disciple Daniels," Kai said.

"Of course. Disciple," Camp greeted pensively.

"My son," Disciple Daniels said. "We got ourselves a problem here."

"We do?" Camp asked, standing with his feet shoulder-width apart and his hands in his pockets. Disciple Daniels chuckled to himself and took another sip from his cup.

"Camp, I want to introduce you to someone special, my uncle," Kai said. She was speaking in a hushed tone and with perfect elocution. What was up with that outfit? "This is my Uncle Fuji. He is a man of influence in New Orleans, South Texas, and the casino districts of Mississippi."

The well-dressed Japanese man set his glass down and bowed slightly.

"Good to meet you, Mr. . . . ." Camp hesitated, trying not to be rude.

"People call me Fuji. Please feel free to do so as well," the man said.

The name triggered remembrances and recollections in Camp's mind.

"Wait, did you say New Orleans? Fuji of New Orleans?" Camp asked, more than a little impressed. "CK, you are related to Fuji Fivepoints?"

"We have some extended family ties. We've settled on uncle and niece," Fuji explained. "Kai called me two days ago, hoping that I might help with developments associated with your business."

Camp looked back and forth from Fuji and Kai to Disciple Daniels.

"Listen, youngblood," Daniels said. "Mr. Fuji and I are part of the same association. The association protects our common secular interests."

"Daniels, I always thought you were in bed with the Russians," Camp said flatly. He didn't want to run afoul of Disciple Daniels, but he didn't like the man. It might have been hypocritical, but a gangster hiding behind the cross just seemed too dark even for him.

"The Russians provide protection and political influence," Kai explained. "However, the association handles the day-to-day aspects of their business."

Camp just nodded and looked back and forth between all the parties.

"Like I was saying, youngblood, we got ourselves a mess here. You and I ain't enemies mainly cause we ain't in the same business or the same area," Daniels explained.

"And I'm backed by the Colombians and the Belize cartels that keep you north of I-20," Camp said.

"And because I don't deal in poison that kills my own people," Daniels said scornfully.

"No, you bankrupt them financially and morally and then hide behind the Holy Ghost," Camp said.

"This is why I am here," Fuji explained. "Mr. Butterfield, the dearly departed Shawn's connection to Brianna, the Disciple's niece, has the potential to put the two of you at odds. And if that happens, it could cause an unnecessary conflict between the Russians and the Colombians."

"So, this is to save the big boys from going to war?" Camp asked.

"Camp, going to war does not benefit anyone. No product moves; no money is made," Kai said softly. Camp looked at her more for how she looked and talked as opposed to what she had said.

Mr. Fuji stepped from behind her and stood between Disciple Daniels and Camp. He was shorter than Camp and maybe fifteen years older. However, he was in excellent shape and impeccably dressed. He explained things so they were crystal clear.

"I am here because I have a connection with you via Kai and an association with Disciple Daniels. I want to broker this meeting to avoid unnecessary conflict. If you don't mind, I will start with you, Mr. Butterfield. Did you know your nephew was involved with Brianna Daniels?"

"Call me, Camp, and no, I did not know. I didn't know Shawn was slipping into town. I definitely didn't know about any baby."

"Is that real talk, Youngblood?" Disciple Daniels asked.

"It's Butterfield to you," Camp said to the old gambler pimp, "but I swear to you I did not know."

"How did you find out?" Disciple Daniels asked.

"My eyes and ears on Atlanta Metro that I have on my payroll," Camp explained.

Disciple Daniels nodded and thought about it for a few seconds. Then he said, "Brianna's mama told me. She's my half-sister; she's still pretty mad at the whole thing."

"Well, Shawn's mother is fucking pissed as well; her son is dead," Camp responded.

Fuji gave Camp a slight nod and a prim smile. He turned to Disciple Daniels.

"I swear on my end that I did not know. If I had, I would have done something about it," Daniels said with a grin straight from the Grinch.

"Something like what?" Camp said. He really did not like this old bastard.

"Like get in touch with you to set him straight," Daniels said. "Youn . . . Butterfield, I don't like this fatal Romeo and Juliet thing these kids were trying, but I did not and would not have shot and killed your nephew or used my police resources to do something so dangerous. It may make good fiction, but it's bad for real life."

Camp watched Disciple Daniels for several seconds. He seemed sincere for the first time today. Camp remembered how the man was a master of longevity. That didn't happen by accident or by making dumb moves.

"So, Cooley doesn't work for you?" Camp asked.

Disciple Daniels shook his head. "The cat seems to be a square deal. Works with little black kids all over the city. And he swears he shot up in the air, not at your nephew."

"Then who shot him?" Camp said.

"Who shot at Cooley two nights ago? And firebombed his house?" Disciple Daniels asked, looking at Camp with a deadpan expression.

"Not me," Camp said.

"The papers say otherwise," Disciple Daniels said. "You can see when it gets out about the baby. Then the papers will start drawing attention to me that I don't need."

"It seems," Fuji interrupted, "we are failing to see all the energy in this conflict. There is clearly another entity at work trying to make a play for Officer Cooley or maybe frame one of you for it."

Camp and Disciple Daniels were quiet for a minute.

"The way my uncle and I see it," Kai said, "one, Shawn was killed accidentally or on purpose, and someone is trying to use it to put Cooley away one way or the other. Two, someone is trying to tie Camp to Cooley's murder or attempted murder. Three, when the news of the baby gets out, that suspicion could spread to Disciple Daniels and his operation. Four, it wasn't us who tried and missed on Cooley. Disciple Daniel says his hands are clean of both Shawn and the Cooley shooting. So, who is trying to move into our territories?"

"What about the Russians?" Camp asked.

Disciple Daniels shook his head.

"I must admit that I have not heard any talk or plans of that," Fuji explained. "Our Russian partners have gotten smarter. They are recognizing the importance of territorial lines to the influx of cash. Wars cost money."

"Our Colombian and Belize partners are the same," Camp said.

The room was quiet, each person thinking the same thing. They were all gangsters, criminals of the highest order. How sure were they of their backers? Camp had achieved his position by pushing out weaker competition with the help of those same backers. Why wouldn't they do it again? Disciple

Daniels was long in the tooth. It was the law of nature to eventually push the old lions out of the pride.

"Camp, my uncle and I have an idea," Kai said in soft, clipped tones.

"Ok?" Camp said

"Disciple Daniels has contacts with Atlanta Metro who can help us with the secret location of Mr. Cooley," Fuji explained.

"They're moving him every four to six hours, but we can find the schedule," Disciple Daniels said. "We can get you in there to talk to Cooley. You can ask him whatever you want, but you can't hurt him and definitely not kill him."

"Talk to him about what?" Camp asked.

"What happened that night? What he saw, what he heard?" Kai explained. "Camp, we got to get to the bottom of what is really happening? Are we victims of circumstance, or is there something else at hand?"

Camp consented. Disciple Daniels stood, as if he were bored with the whole thing.

"I will let you know the time and place," he said, signaling for his two stooges to follow him to the door. "I would suggest that you be very careful about who you share this with . . . as in no one."

Camp thought Daniels was an old, cocky muthafucka, and he couldn't wait to show him out. He watched them until they left. Kai's uncle was talking to her and putting his trench coat on. They turned to Camp as he walked over to them.

"Mr. Fuji, I guess I should thank you," he said.

"You are welcome," Fuji said. "Kai is very special to me. I would do everything in my power to keep her safe."

Kai actually blushed.

As they walked to the door, Fuji turned to Camp. He was serious. For the first time, Camp saw the savvy gangster from New Orleans and not the conciliatory peacemaker.

"A piece of advice, Mr. Butterfield. When we get the address and the time, we need to get Mr. Cooley's family out of your house and back to him. I assume you have done something to secure her silence?"

Camp nodded, wondering how he felt about Fuji knowing about Anousha and Daria. At least he hadn't told that asshole Daniels.

Fuji looked back at Camp Butterfield, wondering if he had used fear or love to secure Mrs. Cooley's silence.

## Chapter Twenty-nine

At about that same time, my phone rang with a number that I hadn't seen on my phone for over two years.

"Blind Billy Brown, is that you?" I asked jovially.

"You better know it before I show it!" Billy said, giving me one of his numerous one-line hip clips. "Is this the Superman they call Lemon Boy?"

Blind Billy Brown was the first and last word in Southern Blues. Pushing eighty years old, he was one of the last living great bluesmen. He'd toured with everyone from Sonny Boy Williamson to BB King. He had songs on motion picture soundtracks and samples on hip hop songs.

In New Orleans, he was the musical force behind the jazz revival that had taken place in the spring. He also owned a small dive club named after him.

"It is. What a good surprise," I said, truly relieved to have some non-business in my life. "What you up to these days? How's N'Orleans?"

"Good when I left her, hot and wet as new coochie and just as fragrant."

"You would know with that hound-dog nose of yours," I said, laughing. I could talk to Blind Billy all day long. He reminded me of my father and his friends back in East St. Louis, the way they talked and joked with each other.

"Listen, Lemon Boy, I'm actually in Atlanta right now. Staying at the Mandarin Oriental."

"Really? So are we; we're all here, including TruLuv."

"I know. That's why I called. Before things get busy today with that football game, I was wondering if we could have a little breakfast over at the Mandarin, say ten o'clock?"

"We always got time for you, Blind Billy. Where you playin' tonight?"

"I'm not; I'm getting an award from Banneker College. They got a pretty good music department. They celebrate all the music, including blues and jazz. Seems I got a pretty strong fan base in those parts."

"Congratulations!" I said, feeling oddly proud of the bluesman that I barely knew but who felt like a long-lost relative.

"Hey, man, I gotta get myself together; it takes us old pimps a minute or two longer than you jackrabbits," he said, laughing at his own humor.

We said our goodbyes, and I went to tell the others.

***

The Mandarin Oriental Hotel is a smaller jewel of opulence amongst the behemoth skyscrapers of downtown Atlanta. Bobby Sr. agreed to stay behind. We had not gotten our call from Bobby Jr., and he was getting worried. He'd sent the operatives out to meet up with the twins and their friends. He'd kept the rest with him if or when Bobby Jr. needed help.

TruLuv, Teri, and I entered the front door of the hotel and

announced ourselves at the registration desk. After checking our IDs, they coded a plastic key card to get us to the floor and room. We were still making jokes about the old blues singer coming up in the world and getting the penthouse on Banneker College's dime when we reached his door.

"There they are!" Billy said as the maid opened the door and we entered the expansive two-bedroom suite with galley kitchen.

The colors were vibrant red, black, gold, and white. The wall portraits were a variety of Chinese, Japanese, and Korean. The furniture was large, overstuffed, and very high-end European.

Each of us hugged the old man as we came by him. He called our names by our shapes and our scents. It was a game Blind Billy used to amuse his friends. He could identify colognes, perfumes, and most lotions and deodorants just by smell. If he got any wrong, I'd never seen it. He was short, about five foot seven inches. His dark skin was still shiny and tight against his face. He had a short afro with salt and pepper hair. He was wearing a royal-blue long-sleeve dress shirt with cufflink sleeves. His black slacks were sharkskin shiny, with the best creases dry cleaning could do. His shoes were original Allen Edmond wingtip oxfords. He wore shades most of the time. Today, he was in a pair of Versace original sunglasses, complete with the gold emblem at the corners of the frames.

We'd met Billy during a life-changing assignment in New Orleans. There had been some local hoods trying to run the blues singer off his blocks after Hurricane Katrina. He'd gotten one of them with his single-edge switchblade. The other one had gotten away.

"It's a perfect morning for sitting out on the terrace," Blind Billy said. "Whatever you need to drink, my helper, Tiera, can get it for us."

"Blind Billy? How are you charging all this to poor little Banneker College?" Teri said, only half-joking.

"Shee, girl, I wouldn't ask anybody to pay for all this," Billy said, taking a glass of something with orange juice from Tiera. She asked orders from the rest of us. We all took water with lemon.

"I'm rolling with Mr. Fuji," he finally explained.

We all let out dubious sighs. Fuji Fivepoints was a sponsor and supporter of Blind Billy's rebuilding of his neighborhood and bar after the hurricane. He was also one of the most feared gangsters in the Southeast United States. He always treated Billy like a dowager grandfather, and I never fully understood what the gangster was getting out of it.

"Is Fuji here?" I asked pensively.

"Uh . . . no . . . he had business on the other side of town," Billy explained. "I imagine he will be out most of the day. But he heard about my coming here, and a few days later, he agreed to upgrade my airline ticket and hotel. Said he wanted me to be sharp when accepting my award at the Chancellors Ball Saturday night after the game."

When Tiera brought our drinks, we strolled across the massive living room to the open sliding glass doors. The openings were covered with a long white semi-sheer curtain that undulated in the morning breeze, which was still cool on the northwest end of the building. Teri took Billy's arm and guided him to the patio/terrace. TruLuv and I walked behind them. Teri reached the opening to the patio, pulled the sheers to the side, and stopped with a stiffening that I picked up on instinctively. I threw my arm in front of TruLuv.

"What is it?" I asked slowly.

"Just more company that arrived before Lemon Boy. We're all friends here, right, Lola baby?"

Billy stepped out onto the terrace pulling Teri with him. I stepped forward, and there she was. Lola was wearing a sleeveless sundress in a muted shade of green. She was sitting on a two-person patio settee, looking out at the skyline with her long brown legs crossed.

After putting my stomach and jaw back in place, it was becoming obvious that Billy's request for the visit was a well-meaning setup. I stepped out onto the expansive patio and realized TruLuv was still inside. I looked back and saw him standing still with a look that was unreadable, but it was aimed right through the patio opening at Lola, his mother, whom he had known as his aunt.

"Listen to me one minute, ok?" Blind Billy said. "Lola didn't know this was going to happen. I tricked her the same way. She was just first to arrive, ok?"

"Are you really getting an award?" Teri asked skeptically.

Billy pulled the folded award letter from his shirt pocket and held it out. Teri just pushed it back for him to put away.

"Lemon, TruLuv, can we just talk for a little bit, just until we finish our drinks, and that's it. Can you do that for old Billy?" he asked.

Blind Billy Brown was a showman until the end. He could be anything from the doddering grandfather to the wily old bluesman with quick hands and a quick wit or anything in between.

I was the first to take a seat in the loveseat right next to her. I had been trying to reach out to her to apologize for Jamaica, where I'd lost it on her. She looked at me and scooted away an inch.

My stare at her was broken when TruLuv plopped down in the seat across from us.

"Hey, Auntie," he said flatly.

"Allen, how are you, baby?" Lola said sweetly.

"Fine, just fine," TruLuv said sarcastically.

"Well, you all got a lot to talk about, so I will wait downstairs," Teri said, turning to leave.

"Or you could stay as well?" Blind Billy asked. "You were the first to discover the truth and bubble it up to the surface. Lemon Boy and Mr. TruLuv respect what you think, value your opinion. You need to be part of the healing."

Teri looked at me, and I motioned for her to take a seat and mouthed the word "Please." Teri sighed and plopped down in a chair next to me. Billy felt and stepped his way to the chair facing her. There was a low cocktail table between us all.

"When I met you all in New Orleans, I had never been around a team so good. You all were good not just because you were talented, but because you love each other. Now, I been knowing this girl since she was in grade school. She ain't evil. She just human. Now, you all are good loving people. All I'm saying is, don't let some short-term hurts rob you of the love you have to give each other."

"I'm cool," Teri said, and everybody rolled their eyes.

"Ok, ok, that man right there?" Teri continued, pointing to me. "He made me everything I am. He believed in me when my own mother and father laughed. I love him like a brother. So, I got a problem when someone plays him."

"I wasn't playin' him," Lola said.

"So, if I had not found out, if we had not run into you in St. Louis, were you ever going to tell him?"

"Yes, but I wanted to tell TruLuv first," Lola said.

"When was that? I was only around you for my whole life. When were you going to tell me I was your son and not your nephew?"

"I was trying to find the right time. I knew it was going to be disruptive, and your career was taking off," Lola explained.

"I can understand it," I said, louder than everyone. "I think I always understood it."

"Even when I first told you?" Lola asked.

"Yeah. I know I didn't act like it. I was hurt," I explained. "But I've had time. Time to get to know my son and for him to get to know me. I've had time to regret some of the things I said to you in the Caribbean. I've tried to reach out to you for the last few months."

"I guess I was hurt too," Lola said. "Even if I deserved to be."

"So, we established one thing," Blind Billy said. "You all got love for each other. You all been hurt, so why can't you all make an attempt to heal?"

SILENCE

"You halfway there," Billy continued. "Lemon Boy and TruLuv seem to be getting along pretty good. Lemon Boy trying to make amends with you, Lola. You're about to make it 1987 up in here again."

That made Lola blush, and she reached her hand over to take mine. I grabbed it and kissed it.

"Now, TruLuv, I know you got at least one of those hippy rap songs that talk about forgiveness and living for today?" Billy goaded.

TruLuv tried to hold his deadpan expression. Then he broke into a grin.

"Yeah, Billy, I think I've rapped about it once or twice," he conceded.

"Think about all the adventures you and Lola shared, the places she took you to, music lessons, tours in Europe, Japan, Korea, and every Caribbean island with a dancehall. She could have taken a whole host of people with her, but she took you," Blind Billy preached.

TruLuv nodded.

"Now imagine her gone tomorrow from a heart attack or plane crash."

"Billy!" Lola said loudly and incredulously.

"Ok, what if the big C comes back and its stage four? Then what you gonna do? Cryin' and snotting at the bedside and jumpin' on coffins, talking about, 'I'm sorry'?"

Those were some cold visuals. The patio suddenly felt like a breezy wasteland. I was sure the slightly sick faces I saw around me only mirrored my own.

"See, even the best of folks get caught up in their own sense of what's important until life hits them over the head with something to make it seem like nothing," Blind Billy continued. "I'm an old man who done seen a lot of misery and regret. I make my living singing 'bout it. I just don't want you all to be the subject of my next album."

"Neither do I, Billy," I said, still holding Lola's hand. "Tru, I appreciate all the space you have made in your heart for me. It ain't been easy, I know. I'm asking you to do the same thing for Lola. If not for her, then I'm asking for me."

By now, TruLuv was crying silent tears, his face a mask of hurt and anger. When he spoke, his voice was high, in a kid's tone, stripped of all his rapper bravado.

"I missed you," he said. "So much. I have been floundering in so many ways for the last year."

Lola just nodded and mumbled her sorry.

"I can try to do what you ask, Pop," he said. "But with some conditions."

"Of course," Lola said.

"I am sooo fucking mad at you and will be for a while," he said.

"That's fair, and you need to tell her every time you feel that way," Blind Billy said.

"Oh, I will. Next, you got to work on more than just my forgiveness. There's trust, reliance . . . "

"Allen, please just give me a chance," Lola pleaded, getting up from her seat and walking closer to TruLuv. "And we can make it just like it used to be."

"No, you can never do that. That was a beautiful life based on a lie," TruLuv said, residual bitterness lacing his tearful voice, "but that don't mean we can't build something good."

Lola nodded and moved the rest of the way, her arms outstretched. TruLuv allowed himself to be engulfed in her embrace. Anyone on that patio could see how much they needed each other and fit into each other's lives. I got up and walked silently over to them. I placed my hand on TruLuv's back and patted him as he continued to sob into Lola's embrace like a kid reunited with his family after a kidnapping. Lola caught my attention and mouthed her thank you. I turned to Teri, who was sitting in her chair, looking down at the drink in her hand.

"How about it, Teri?" I said. "You want me to be happy? Well, here it is?"

She nodded and smiled solemnly.

"I'm always down, Darryl. Whatever, whenever," she said.

## Chapter Thirty

The Fighting Lions of Birmingham A&M were on amp and surge. Transported from the hotel to the dome stadium in luxury buses, they stepped off into a media storm. Atlanta metro police and Georgia highway patrol maintained a column of screaming, yelling fans eager to get a look and a picture of the players. Every sports outlet was represented. Independent sports bloggers were also there.

KeeVon was in a black Gucci tuxedo coat, matching trousers, and a monochrome gold shirt and tie. He was wearing gold high-top LeBron sneakers.

His hair was fresh out the shop, with natural texture and a straight-razor lining. He face was clean-shaven save for the tuft of chin hair that was part of his good-luck ritual. He had on gold-rimmed, retro-styled Foster Grant shades that his mother, Madina, had said were a bit too Hollywood. However, he kept the gold wireless headphones on his ears. As he smiled and waved to the crowd, all he could hear in his ear was DJ Khalid's "All I Do Is Win."

The Banneker College team chose to come in a different way. Before getting off the bus, they donned their game jerseys. Then, after lining up four in each row, they locked arms and walked in, chanting, "Hey, hey, hey, goodbye!" No smiles, no waves. All business. The crowd loved it.

Inside the rehearsal hall, the bands were in mid-dress, going over last-minute adjustments and routines. That was where Medina found Gina Pombo with the other Marching Pride drum majors. Gina had left a message that she needed to see her. Fearing that Gina was experiencing some type of retaliation, Madina had come down to the rehearsal hell bent for leather. She was wearing a sable gold suede pantsuit. It was obviously custom made, fitting her like a model.

"Hey, G! What's up? You need something?" Madina said, looking around, on alert.

"I'm good," Gina said, but she said it solemnly. "Can we talk in private?"

They walked over to an unoccupied portion of the rehearsal hall.

"I just wanted to say I appreciate all that you've done for me. Last night was a dream come true," Gina said.

"You earned it. You worked your ass off, and when you got your chance, you brought down the house. Now, I'm busy, baby. I got a house to bring down myself in a few hours today with this game and concert. Talk to me."

Gina Pombo wrapped her hands together and then pushed forward with her request.

"I want to ask for Milton to perform today," she said quickly. When Madina looked as surprised as she had feared she would, she continued.

"I promise that I will still file charges against him, but this is THE biggest event in the history of the Marching Pride Band. He may be a prick asshole who hates women, but he is the best we have. He's earned that title."

"I hear you," Madina said with the smile of an indulgent mother talking to a naïve child, "but this sounds like guilt."

Gina shook her head.

"Or pressure from your peers?"

Gina shook her head no.

"Or worry that you can't hold your own for the rest of the season and they will blame you?"

"NO!" Gina said, partly out of frustration and partly from the audacity of Madina's questions.

"Ms. Sherman, you told me to live my truth and not apologize. Well, you gotta understand something about the drum major corp. We stick together no matter what. We piss each other off; we step on each other's toes . . ."

"You sexually assault each other?" Madina said.

"As to that," Gina said, "the law will decide what his punishment will be, but this is another thing. This is drum major code. I want to be true to that even if people don't get it."

Madina didn't like it, but she got it. It made her admire this little powerhouse even more.

"Ok," Madina said. "You got it. The little asshole can go on the field. I'll let Dr. Tolliver know, and I will let them both know that it is happening because of you."

They hugged for a long time.

"Now, I gotta go," Madina said. "Good luck out there."

As Gina turned to walk away, Madina lightly smacked her on the back as if to say, "Knock 'em dead."

When Gina returned to the rest of the band, she didn't say anything. About an hour later, she heard the room erupt in happy chatter. She turned to see Milton strolling into the rehearsal hall, his uniform on his shoulder. He shook hands all around. The official story was that he was sick, a contagious virus of some kind. Now he was feeling better and going to perform. According to Dr. Tolliver, he was to stay away from Gina except for their performance on the field. When he worked his way through the crowd and was a few feet away, he made eye contact with her. She gave him a brief nod. He returned the nod, his face an emotionless mask.

"You ready? Feeling good?" Jesse Isaacs said behind her. Gina turned around. He was standing there, a pleading, sorrowful look on his face.

"I'm good. Thanks for asking."

"Last night was crazy; your performance was fire!" he said. This was the third or fourth time she had heard it from him. "Gina, I just wanted to say that I know. Milton was drunk last night. I checked on him after the battle. He told me what happened."

"How much did he tell you?" she asked, feeling a little sick.

"Not too much. He was trying to justify himself, but I was able to read through his lies."

"I can't really talk about that today."

"I just wanted to say to you that I did not know what he was doing. I promise I didn't. I was around the guy for almost three years, and I had no clue."

"Ok," Gina said flatly.

"I wanted to say I was sorry and that going forward, I will be a better bandmate."

"Thanks, Jesse. I will settle for this. We'll look out for each other the way Butta looked out for all of us."

## Chapter Thirty-one

David Cooley was being moved every four hours to different houses around the city and county. He was safe, but he was worried sick about his wife and child.

In the last forty-eight hours, he had been shot at and had caused the death of that poor woman from the church and painful injury to Father Burke. For the first twenty-four hours, he had no idea what had happened to his wife and daughter. His mind had been filled with the worst thoughts.

Then he got a message from his in-laws telling him that Anousha and Daria were safe. They didn't have any additional news. David wondered if they were telling the truth. He had never been their favorite person. They swore it was not because he was white, but he was not so sure.

He wondered if Anousha and Daria were with them and if they were just lying to him. He had to believe that if that were the case, his wife would have reached out to him.

It was noon on Saturday. They were in transport to the Virginia Highland area. His main handlers were a couple of thirty-year veterans named Levy and Taylor. This location was a three-story house just north of Orme Park on Brookridge Drive.

"This place is pretty nice," Taylor said. "They even had a decent supply of hooch the last time we were here."

Cooley wondered how the police department owned or had access to all these houses. This was the fifth one since the shooting at the church. Even though they hadn't hit him, he'd felt the weight of guilt from the poor priest, who would need facial reconstruction and a healthy dose of mental health rehab. He had just shaken hands with poor Mrs. Gernst, who had eventually died from her gun wounds. Deep inside, he felt that whoever they were, they would eventually get him. Maybe that would be better than dying in prison.

They climbed the massive front stairs to the Victorian porch. In a few seconds, they were in the foyer. It was dark save for the daylight coming through the elaborate antique stained-glass window.

"Daddy!" came a child's voice from the back of the house.

For a couple of seconds, David Cooley thought he was hallucinating. He continued to feel surreal until Daria jumped into his arms.

"Dar! what are you doing here? Where is your mother?" he asked. Holding her, he turned to look at Levy and Taylor, but they had slipped out the front door.

By this time, Daria was crying, and he was soothing her. He moved through the house. It was well decorated in Victorian wallpaper, rugs, and furnishings. When he got to the formal dining room, Anousha was standing there with her eyes full of tears. She was running into his arms when he finally noticed the others in the room.

There was another police officer, a well-dressed Asian guy, one well-dressed older black guy who looked familiar, and a mixed-race person that he was pretty sure was a woman dressed in man's clothes. He thought this should be weird, but so much weirdness had happened in the last week.

"We're good, Dennis," the black guy said. The police officer gave a two-finger salute. He left the dining room and headed to the front of the house. David watched him sit in the front room and begin to read the newspaper.

"Mr. Cooley, we'd like a word," the black guy said. He was well dressed in a navy three-piece suit. He introduced himself as Disciple Daniels. David did not immediately recognize him. This could have been due to his relatively short time on the force.

"Ok, what is this about? Where is my detail?" he asked, feeling a setup. After everything that had happened to him, along with the disappearance and reappearance of his family, he refused to be surprised by anyone.

Just then, Camp Butterfield came out of the kitchen. He was holding a coffee pot in one hand and dangling five cups from each finger on the other hand. When David Cooley saw him, he pushed Anousha and Daria behind him and backed out of the room, towards the front of the house.

"Mr. Cooley, relax," Disciple Daniels implored. "We are only here to talk."

"I'm not a fool, Daniels; I know who that this," David said.

"Daddy, that's Marques; he's a fireman!" Daria said.

The entire room looked at Daria and then back to Camp.

"It's true," Camp said in a soft whisper as he slowly set the coffee pot and cups down on the table. "We just here to talk. I'm not armed, so let's not alarm the D-baby and Noush."

"I believe 'em, babe; let's hear 'em out," Anousha said softly, standing behind him.

They all sat around the large dining room table. David and Anousha, with Daria on her lap, sat on one side. Camp, Kai, and Fuji sat on the other side. Disciple Daniels sat at the head of the table. The tension was as heavy as a wet steel blanket. David still felt the specter of death near him. Camp felt the specter of arrest and prison sitting in a police safe house. Anousha felt her secrets swimming around the room, looking for an inconvenient place to land.

In the background, Daria was humming to herself and singing softly while playing with a Tiana doll.

"First, I did not shoot at you in front of the church. I did not shoot that priest or that old lady," Camp said defiantly.

"No, you were firebombing my house," David snapped back.

"No, I didn't," Camp replied. "Think about it. Why would I bomb your house and shoot at you in front of the church?"

"Simple, you wanted to wipe out my entire family. You think I killed your family, so you wanted to return the favor."

"Yet you are all sitting here," Disciple Daniels interjected.

"So, for brutal honesty, you been watching my house?" David asked.

Camp started to protest, but Kai broke into the conversation. "Yes, we were watching your home. I also followed you to the church. I was there when the other shooter was firing on you."

"And you were just curious about me? Or was the idea to kill me at some point?" David asked.

Kai hesitated. She glanced at Fuji and Camp and then nodded.

"And yet we are all still here," Disciple Daniels repeated.

"It is obvious there are others out there trying to kill you, maybe your family as well. That gives us pause," Kai said. "Maybe whoever is going after you also has destructive designs on our business and even that of Disciple Daniels here."

"Ok, I'm going to apologize for this question up front," David said. "Disciple Daniels, are you a gangster? Like Mr. Butterfield?"

"Disciple Daniels has financial interests in certain enterprises whose revenue streams co-mingle with those of Mr. Butterfield," Fuji explained.

"I take that as a yes," David said, smiling and shaking his head. "So, now what?"

Still sensing death was just over his shoulder, he felt defeated and tired. His only concern was getting Anousha and Daria out alive. He was past thinking he would live long enough to make it to trial.

The rest of the room sat back in their chairs and, still looking pensive, took sips of their coffee.

"First, I need to hear it from you everything that happened that night," Camp explained calmly. "Somebody at least owes me that."

The room was quiet for almost a minute.

"I was substituting in the CNN Precinct with three other officers. Takeshi and I were from precincts north and east. McGill and Brody were from that area, and—"

"Stop!" Camp practically shouted. "McGill and Brody were with you when you shot Butta?"

"I did not shoot your cousin; I shot into the air!" David shouted back. He was sick of saying it, sick of being called a closet bigot, sick because, despite the certainty of his aim, he could not explain what had happened to Shawn the night he died.

"Camp, just hear him out, please?" Anousha said.

Camp sat down and motioned for David to continue. After a pause, he did.

"Takeshi and I were in one mobile unit north of Centennial Park. Brody and McGill were at the south end. There had been a briefing about robberies and assaults in and around Centennial Park. Then Shawn was spotted running through the park. Brody said he tried to stop him but couldn't catch him or get his attention. He was wearing earbuds. McGill or Brody, not sure which one, suggested we cut him off at the next cross street. About that time, he shot past us, running across Baker Avenue, north into Pemberton Pavilion, between the Coke Museum and the Georgia Aquarium. Takeshi took off after him. I pursued in the mobile to the next east-west thoroughfare, Ivan Allen Boulevard.

"I got out of the squad car and stood near the Center for Human and Civil Rights. When I saw Shawn, he was running north, but more northeast, on an angle away from me. I called for Takeshi but got no answer. I confirmed that I had sight of Shawn but couldn't catch him. He was really moving. McGill or Brody suggested making a warning shot in the air to get his attention. I thought that was pretty extreme, especially since we had no evidence that he was doing anything wrong. He was just a kid running through the park and the pavilion late at night.

"I tried running after him, but he was getting farther and farther away. McGill was shouting for me not to let him get past Ivan Allen and into the apartment complexes because we would never catch him. I finally stopped, shouted for him to stop, and fired straight into the air. I shot up, two shots, and he went down like he'd run into a wall."

David finished his story, his eyes full of bewildered sorrow.

"We just wanted to stop him and ask him where he was going running through that area at that time of night."

"Officer Cooley, what happened immediately after the shooting? Where were your fellow officers?" Fuji asked.

"Takeshi came running up almost a minute later; said he had to stop and catch his breath. Brody and McGill about fifteen minutes later."

"Where the hell were they?" Kai asked. She had the area pulled up on GPS. "If they were coming from the south end of Centennial Park, it should not have taken that long."

"I . . . I never thought about it," David said, thinking back on the incident. "I was trying to staunch the bleeding and calling 911. Takeshi was working crowd control."

The room was silent for another minute. Camp spoke first.

"Then it's true that Butta was just running through the park when he got shot."

"I swear, Mr. Butterfield, I did not shoot your cousin. I fired up in the air. Looking back on it, I probably shouldn't have done it. We could have just let him go, but McGill and Brody were shouting and pushing us to stop him. You say you didn't firebomb the house, and I guess I have to believe you."

"Daddy, MB didn't firebomb our house," Daria said. "He's a fireman."

"I know, Daria," David said.

"I know who firebombed our house because I saw him," Daria said.

The room went silent, and all eyes turned to the child sitting in Anousha's lap.

"How did you see him?" David asked. "Tell Daddy everything you saw."

"I was going to the kitchen to get water before bath time, but then I had to go to the bathroom. I was in the bathroom, and I heard a crash like glass." Daria clenched both of her tiny fists and made her eyes big as she told the story. "I tiptoed out of the bathroom, and the hallway was full of smoke, and the front door was lying on the floor. Then there was another crash, and I got scared and called Mama. Then I saw him. He was standing in the front yard. He was holding a beer bottle with fire coming out of it."

"Did he see you?" David asked her.

Daria shook her head.

"I hid behind the bathroom door. He was standing there, looking at the windows like he was looking for somebody, so I hid. Then he ran to his truck and drove away." She punctuated the last statement with a wave of her arm to simulate a vehicle taking off at high speed.

"What about . . . MB?" David said, referencing Daria's name for Camp.

"I went back into the bathroom because I figured Mama would be coming to get me and would be mad if I was walking on the glass," she said very casually. "I heard a car pull up, and I thought it was you, Daddy, so I came out of the bathroom, and MB was standing there in the front yard. He saw me and came in and got me. He took me outside. Then he went to get Mama. She was sleeping, so he had to carry her. That was it."

"And then you went to his house?" David asked.

"Yep, we had spaghetti and chocolate chip cookies, and, and, and . . ." She stopped short.

"And what, Daria? What else?" David asked, worried. Daria continued to look guiltily at Camp and then back to her father.

"Um . . . we had sugar cereal," she admitted, looking at her shoes. David sighed and chuckled to himself. He looked at Camp, who smiled.

"Captain Crunch, a classic," he said.

"And it was good too," Daria said, and the entire room chuckled.

"Is there anything else you need, Camp? Our window is closing here. We need to get moving," Disciple Daniels said.

Camp was punching into his phone. When he found what he wanted, he turned the screen so Daria could see it. Seeing the picture on the screen, she nodded and shrank into her mother's arms.

"I'm done," Camp said, standing with new energy.

They left David Cooley with his family.

## Chapter Thirty-two

"Today, we take this field to continue our march!" Coach McMullen said. "Our Sherman's March. Today, Banneker College. Tomorrow, the HBU Championship!"

The team roared back. KeeVon Sherman was right in the front. The Fighting Lions of Birmingham A&M were in their gold and black, ready for battle. They had been on a tear, defeating every opponent by double digits. The entire team had gotten behind KeeVon's campaign to break as many records and earn a spot on the top ten sports highlights on ESPN and Fox Sports Network.

"I know this seems like a unique experience, the media storm, the size of the crowd, the swag bags, the fancy hotel rooms, and the high-end grub! But at the end of the day, it's still A&M against Banneker, the Pride against the Bruins. Don't get sidetracked by all this other crap. Understood?"

Nods all around.

"And on that same point, I have personally read some disturbin' Facebook posts and Instagram messages about having some kind of kneeling protest by the players during this game. I have talked to Coach Cade of Banneker College, and we have assured each other, along with the administrators and event organizers, that there will be no kneeling during the National Anthem. Is that clear?"

"Yes, Coach!"

"This ain't the NFL! This is Lion Pride Nation!"

"Yes, Coach!"

The field was electric. Both bands were in the stands, playing with swagger and style. Temporary platforms had been built in front of the band for the drum majors to do their thing. The dome stadium holds about eighty thousand, and by game time, thanks to Madina's marketing machine, every seat was sold. She was standing in the executive booth with the school administrators, the executives from the conference, the stadium management, and major advertisers. She was all smiles; she was bringing it off.

Both teams came out of the tunnels at the same time. This had been timed for television. Madina wanted a monstrous cheer. Network television set up a sound sensor that showed the loudness of the crowd in decibels. The sound meter ripped past a hundred decibels, held at 106, and hovered there as the crowds roared continuously.

Before going to their respective sides, both teams, over a hundred players, hustled to the fifty-yard line. Before the coaches could say anything, the players knelt as if to pray. The crowd appreciated the gesture, cheering throughout. The coaches didn't like surprises, but they chose to let it go for now. Ethan Cobb, the kicker for Banneker College and the son and grandson of ministers, led the prayer. He stood in the middle of the massive huddle of kneeling players. Then, just after the end of the prayer, while they were still in a kneeling, praying posture, over a hundred black-gloved fists rose in the air. They stood, counted off to three, and then shouted,

"BUTTA! BUTTA! BUTTA!"

The teams separated to their respective sidelines, still chanting the dead drum major's name. The bands were the first to pick up on the chant, then the undergrad section, then the rest of the crowd. For twenty seconds, the entire stadium was chanting, "Butta," which forced the commentator for the national network broadcast feed to explain its purpose. Now the story about Shawn Butterfield was nationwide.

"Sherman!" Coach McMullen shouted at the star quarterback when he returned to the sideline. KeeVon was taking congratulations from his team. He broke off because he knew this was coming.

"We had to do something, Coach. We just had to. We promise not to demonstrate on the anthem."

"Yeah, but you cut our warmup time short," Coach said, only half mad.

"But it's cut short for both teams," KeeVon said.

Coach couldn't argue with that. He held up a cell phone. "You know who wants a word," he said and walked away.

"Hey, Mama," KeeVon said. He was expecting the mother of all cursing.

"Tell me that is all the surprises you little negroes have in store for me today," she said in an eerily calm voice.

"Yes, that's it. I promise. Mama, I—"

"No, no, don't talk. Just listen. What you did was not part of the plan, and the networks were nervous, but sometimes, it's better to be lucky than good. The fact that you did this before the National Anthem is trending good on social media. As long as you got nothing else up your sleeve, I can spin this."

"I promise, Mama," he said, relieved that she was not mad.

"Personally, I'm proud of what you guys did. It made ME cry."

"Whaaaaa . . ." he said. "I don't believe it."

"Shut up, boy, and make me a believer on that field. Kick some Banneker ass."

When he hung up, Coach McMullen asked, "What did she say?"

KeeVon put his helmet on and snapped his chinstrap. "Mama said knock 'em out!"

I didn't see the player's tribute to Butta in real time. Teri and her operatives were with TruLuv in the dome, getting ready for halftime. Bobby Sr. and I were with Captain Sayles and his men.

The familiar face I'd pulled out of the bathroom ceiling the night before had turned out to be a member of the New Revolutionaries, the militant black group we had been tracking on the dark web. After some time, stadium security had caught two more stuck in a narrow portion of the attic crawlspace. After a cutting torch had been used to extricate them, they'd been willing to confess to everything as far back as skipping school in the eighth grade. We had earned a certain amount of street credibility with Captain Sayles. So, when we told him about our man undercover with the Pure American Posse, he let us tag along on the surveillance detail.

Our remaining operatives were on the field, playing lookout for the police.

And what were we seeking? A 1970s white cargo van with Baldwin County license plates and a magnet sign for waste removal. If that wasn't enough, the transponder in Bobby Jr.'s boot would be enough.

At that moment, Bobby Jr. was in the back of the smelliest vehicle he had ever experienced. He had been sitting amongst these rednecks who called themselves the Pure American Posse. He didn't know what was going to get him first, the rotten food, the constant snuff chewing, the non-existent hygiene, or just the smell. His father was worried and had wanted him pulled out after the night in the alley with the twins, but he needed to stay. They had been talking about a big show of force on game day. He had to stick around to see what they were planning.

What had started off as placing bombs around the stadium had changed to kidnapping football players. Then it had become the present plan: to find a group of unsuspecting protesters and plow through them.

The night before, there had been long discussions about driving routes and even which protesters to target. The twins had come up in the conversation. Then the Wild Turkey and skunkweed had come out, and things had gotten fuzzy like they always did. They were staying in a vacant house under construction in Lawrenceville. The water was running, but they'd somehow hacked the digital electric meter.

This morning, they were hung over and moving through the crowd on Northside Drive, which led to the dome.

"There it is!" Bobby Sr. said. My partner was more nervous than you will ever see a grizzled old Irish cop from St. Louis be. We were sitting in the Atlanta Metro surveillance van, but Bobby Sr. was using his equipment. The transponder in Bobby Jr.'s boot was the best money could buy. He had gotten himself put in charge of the vehicle's disguise, so he knew exactly how it would look. He texted the details to us earlier that morning. Two nights ago, we'd been ready to pass them off as a bunch of druggies who couldn't pull off a trip to get gas, much less make an attack on the public. The thing Bobby Jr. couldn't figure out was who was financing them. Despite their squatter status, supplies, food, weed, liquor, and chewing tobacco showed up in abundance on a daily basis. When he asked the crowd about it, they got touchy and quiet. Sensing something bigger here, he decided to mole in and see how the land lay.

Bobby Sr. hated these undercover assignments. He worried endlessly, although he would never admit it. The truth was that Bobby Jr. was good at it. He had an all-American face and an athletic build that he wasn't afraid to use, and for a millennial, he was fairly adaptable to a wide range of circumstances and living conditions. I think on some level he enjoyed playing the roles.

Soon after Bobby Sr. found the transponder blip on his tracker software, the white van nosed into the bumper-to-bumper traffic about two blocks from the dome stadium. The call went out to all police field units to be sharp and ready to respond. We sent the same to our operatives in the field. What happened next was a total shocker.

Buddy Grandelle, the lesser-known offspring of the Virginia Grandelles, was driving the van. He could follow directions as long as he mumbled them out loud to himself. Then he saw a bunny and got distracted. The bunny was one of my operatives, a big California surfer type named Kelly, who wore his blonde hair in a ponytail when on the job.

We would find out later that when Buddy saw Kelly, he remembered him from the skirmish in the alley. Marvin Grandelle hadn't been able to teach his son much, but had did instilled in him the urge to never to back down from a fight until you had won. Seeing his chance to get back at Kelly and all those with him, Buddy did not wait for the go signal and drove straight at him as he was standing amongst a crowd about one block away from the dome stadium.

To his credit, Kelly saw it coming and started moving people out of the way. The old white van veered left and bounced up on the curve, following him. Captain Sayles's men went into action. The sea of tailgaters parted with agile quickness. Buddy was on automatic pilot, screaming, "I'm gone git you, sucka'!" Bobby Jr. and the rest of the good old boys in the back were tossed around like wet laundry in a dryer. When the first one started to throw up, the rest followed suit. Soon, the car was full of cursing, bouncing bodies and vomit. In the end, Buddy didn't hit anything but some barbeque grills and a tree, which eventually caused his stop. By then, Bobby Jr. and the rest were falling out of the back, coughing and gagging. They surrendered easily and without incident. Buddy, who went running after Kelly, was later found unconscious at the feet of some alumni members of the Omega Psi Phi fraternity. They disavowed laying a hand on him, saying they'd found him like that.

Atlanta Metro made quick work of the van and the "posse." The plan was to let Bobby Jr. get arrested with the rest and then get him out sometime later. We didn't want his cover blown and have a nation of bigoted idiots coming after him. Even white supremacists have discovered the internet.

AS they were dragged away, he made eye contact with his dad and gave him a wink. Then he fell back into character and made a feigned threat about "whipping the old cripple's ass for looking at me funny."

Bobby Sr. was so relieved that his son was safe that he laughed at the remark.

The tailgating continued as normal. The fairgrounds outside the stadium was awash in fraternity and sorority colors, the aroma of meat cooking, and forty years of good black music. I could swear it seemed organized by decades. There was a section that could only have been called "the Dirty South," playing everything Atlanta had ever produced, from OutKast to T.I. to Jermaine Dupri. Everyone was in Halloween costumes in honor of the Big Boo Classic.

 A little farther into the crowd, some ladies of Delta Sigma Theta were decked out in their colors, relaxing and laughing while Mary J. Blige sang about being happy. Teri let her window down and gave the call. They responded, throwing up the hand sign. There was a bunch of men doing all the barbequing and arguing about charcoal.

Farther into the tailgating area, Kappas and Omegas who looked as old as me were showing younger versions of themselves how to step. Parliament Funkadelic was who they'd chosen to listen to. Some of them were wearing Black Panther masks from the motion picture.

There were the ladies of Alpha Kappa Alpha and the men of

Alpha Phi Alpha being served by some poorly dressed young ladies doing the work. Teri explained they were pledges coming to the end of their time "on line." It seemed a damn mess, and I made a note to ask her about her days pledging. They were playing Chicago house music.

There were Sigma men enjoying what looked like a crab boil with the ladies of Zeta Phi Beta. Both groups had flags eight feet tall. They were playing New Orleans bounce music.

Sigma Gamma Rho ladies were frying fish and hosting a card party with the men of Iota Phi Theta. The music appeared to be the classics. When we drove by, I could hear Earth, Wind & Fire's "September."

Then there were others, local Atlanta folks. They also wore Halloween costumes, from motion picture monsters to sexy pirates. They were in Falcons, Hawks, and Braves t-shirts and jerseys. It was a beautiful scene. The Big Boo Classic was going to happen, and it was going to be a hit. I wondered what Madina was doing at that very moment.

## Chapter Thirty-three

In the end, Birmingham A&M won in overtime, 20–17. KeeVon put on a show and added a lot of running and passing yards to his stats, but Banneker College had a defense with a mob mentality. It would bend, but it would not break. There were several goal-line stances where KeeVon came up short on scoring. It came down to a field goal by a freshman kicker named Marius Refugio from Puerto Rico. He had never played American football before this year. Coach McMullen had seen how he kicked a soccer ball and decided to try him. It turned out to be good luck all around.

After the game, I found the twins and their friends in the stands. I'd expressly asked them that they not protest during the game. They got a chance to meet KeeVon Sherman. They told him how much they appreciated the tribute on the field. KeeVon said he remembered seeing them in the protest crowds.

"From Ferguson, St. Louis, right?" he asked as he gave each of them a one-handed dap hug.

They all made a pledge to keep up the fight and never forget.

By the time we made it back out onto the fairgrounds outside the dome, I remembered why I'd wanted the twins and their friends to go inside.

The president of the United States had decided on that very

weekend to hold another concert of the True America on the same night as the concert to end the Big Boo Classic. When we came out of the stadium, we saw two stages set up side by side, each for the different events. It was a recipe for disaster. Atlanta Metro and Georgia State Park Service had set up a temporary chain-link fence that ran perpendicular to the stages and divided the listening audience. The Big Boo Classic headline act was Lola Montclaire, my Lola. The True America Concert headline artist was Tommi B.

No one was more confused than the public. They milled around the fence, going back and forth on either side. There were new arrivals who hadn't tailgated or gone to the game. They were wondering what this was. Something told me I needed to stick around backstage. I'd kept two operatives with me even though Lola had her own security.

In a few minutes, the bands came up on stage. They started their individual intro songs. It was musical noise. However, both bands continued to play for about two more minutes. Then Lola and Tommi B came on stage at the exact same time, wearing the same dress. The bands stopped. They both found their microphones.

"Good evening, everybody!" Lola started. "This is a crazy setup, right?"

The crowd from both sides applauded.

"You know, whoever put this together doesn't know a damn thing about a good concert," Tommi B said.

"Right, this seems to have been put together by somebody who wants to cause confusion, bad feelings, and conflict."

"Well, we been in the business way too long to let that happen, right, Lola?"

"MMMM-Hmmm."

Then they turned to their respective bands and counted it off together, "One, two, three!"

Both bands broke into the same music, playing in unison.

"So, here is how this will work," Lola said. "We're going to have an old-fashioned dueling band concert. I will sing one; then Tommi B will sing one. At the end of the night, guess who wins?"

Both crowds cheered at the prospect.

For the next ninety minutes, the two queens of eighties and nineties pop sang songs from their catalog and covered other Billboard Top Forty hits. They even sang each other's songs just to be cheeky. Between songs, they joked and jived with each other. They pitted their bands against each other, guitar against guitar, drums against drums, and horns against horns.

By the time they finished, the crowds were cheering for both singers. It was something I had seen Lola do hundreds of times, totally control a crowd and have them eating out of her hand. However, I was always amazed at watching it done. It was supernatural. She came off the stage feeling electric. She saw me at the rear of the backstage area and blew me a kiss.

The concert was a smashing success. Their managers were discussing the idea of a Dueling Diva Concert series.

## Chapter Thirty-four

The autumn Sunday morning over Atlanta was glorious. The sun shone brightly, and there was a cool breeze that seemed to come straight from the north Georgia Mountains. The old folks standing outside the Emory Concert Hall for the Big Boo Classic's Gospel Fest said they could taste cooler weather in the air. It was the final event for the weekend, and it was not televised. Not that Madina couldn't sell the time slot, given the musical guests she'd booked. However, there was something that told her this should be like the other classics. Either you came and experienced it, or you missed it until next year.

Like most of the big gospel events in town, Dancing Disciple Daniels was on the agenda to say a "few" words. Before all that came the parade of hats.

Ladies were in their finest church attire, topped off with exquisite headwear. There were brims so wide you couldn't see their faces and petite pillbox versions so delicately made that they looked like deserts. And of course, there were hats in every color of the rainbow.

In the backstage offices, an important meeting was taking place. Disciple Daniels, his half-sister, Justine, and her daughter, Brianna, were in a green room usually reserved for artists and musical acts resting before going on stage. A few minutes later, they were joined by Camp Butterfield and Rita Butterfield, his aunt and Shawn's mother. The ladies did not know each other, but it was high time they met.

"I understand you pregnant and it's my Shawn's baby," Rita

said.

"That's right," Justine said.

"I want to hear it from her, if it's all the same to you," Rita said not unkindly.

"Well, it might not be—" Justine started to say, but Brianna cut her mother off.

"It's ok, Mama."

Brianna told the whole story, about how they'd known each other, how he'd won her heart, and the plans they had made. She confirmed in front of her mother that Shawn had not been doing business with his cousin any longer. She had copies of all his semester grades and his letters confirming his selection to the dean's list.

Rita wept silently, like she had done so many times over the last eight days.

"I don't want any bad blood between us," she said. "Brianna seems like a fine girl. She would have to be for Shawn to go through what he did to be with her."

"Thank you," Justine said. "I guess I was wrong about some of the things I thought as well."

"But this baby. My Shawn's baby. I want to be a part of that life."

"Of course," Brianna said. "And the baby will be a Butterfield, if that's okay."

Rita just nodded with happiness as the tears streamed down her face.

"I think it's only right," Disciple Daniels said. "Just looks more proper."

Brianna looked back at her mother, who nodded.

"Ms. Butterfield," Brianna asked. "Would you sit with us at the Gospel Fest? We're family now."

## Chapter Thirty-five

On Monday, Atlanta was back to its hustling, bustling way of life. The classic ads were replaced with the upcoming Falcons home game against the Buccaneers. Birmingham A&M and Banneker College students were back on campus, attending classes and preparing for their next opponents. Madina was somewhere banking her percentage of the fees and beating the bushes for the next PR opportunity for her, KeeVon, and his 3G brand leading up to the NFL draft in six months.

Paladin Security was ready to leave town, but Captain Sayles called us Sunday night and asked us to stay to help out with the Shawn Butterfield investigation. Tuesday morning, we met in a meeting room at, of all places, the Mandarin Oriental.

Bobby Sr., Bobby Jr., Teri, and I peeked in and were introduced to Detective Howard, whom we had met last week. The rest included Captain Sayles, a nattily dressed older African-American man called Disciple Daniels, the infamous Camp Butterfield, one of Camp's associates, named Cadillac Kai Davis, and our old friend from New Orleans, Fuji Fivepoints. There were also two older gentlemen sitting on either side of Camp Butterfield. By the cut of their suits, stern expressions, and old-fashioned but expensive briefcases, they were obviously attorneys.

"There is a distinct possibility that Shawn Butterfield was shot by rogue cops in an attempt to remove Camp Butterfield from his spot in the Morolta crime organization," Captain

Sayles explained.

The team and I looked at Camp Butterfield at the end of the table. He just stared at the table in front of him.

After all the protests and counter-protests, after all the accusations of bigotry and minority entitlement, it appeared that both sides had been only half right about the real enemies.

"How can we help?" I asked. "My client, TruLuv, knew Shawn well. We all want to see justice."

That was the only time Camp Butterfield acknowledged our presence with a congenial nod.

In the end, we helped by doing what we do. Security.

Not knowing who to trust, Captain Sayles put Paladin in charge of guarding the hunted Officer David Cooley and his family. TruLuv and the twins had left town about forty-eight hours earlier. This made things easier for what was to come.

The Cooley package was now housed at The Trilogy Hotel, located near Inman Park. It was a square building on the corner on the south end of historic downtown. There was a four-story parking garage across the street. For all practical purposes, it was the worse place to provide protection, and that was the point. The only unknown was how long we would have to stay there.

When they did come, it was no surprise. David Cooley was sitting in the third-floor window that faced the garage. Well-known detectives had purposely been seen going in and out of the hotel right through the front door. If they were watching, we wanted there to be no mistake that Cooley was here.

There were three Paladin operatives in the garage, one on each floor except the first. Captain Sayles's men, dressed in plain clothes, were with them. Bobby Sr. was the one in disguise for a change, dressed as a homeless veteran. He was parked in his chair in front of a gastropub across the street from the hotel and next door to the parking garage. Teri and Bobby Jr. were behind the desk with the actual front-desk clerk.

At 11:32 PM, there was a pinging off the window just behind David Cooley's head. The second and third shot broke the hotel window but pinged off the self-standing bulletproof glass panel inside the room, just behind the real window. One shot embedded in the bulletproof panel. The other ricocheted off the panel and off of two other surfaces in the room.

"I got 'em, Lem," Bobby Sr. said over the common communicator line. "I caught the flash and laser trace. Third floor of the parking garage, west end."

"Got it. Garage units moving," Captain Sayles said. He was on the floor of the hotel room, kneeling over David Cooley, who had dived for the floor and ducked from the window when the glass window had broken.

"Copy that! We'll cover the garage exit if the shooter makes it that far," Bobby Sr. said.

Things remained that way for about six seconds. Then the other shoe dropped.

"Shots fired in the west stairway!" Teri said over the common communicator. "Second shooter in the building!"

Seconds later, the hotel room burst open.

He came in wearing a winter ski mask and hiding behind a housekeeper. She was in her fifties, with hard blond hair with gray streaks. She had a look of abject terror on her pale, bloodless face. Her mouth was moving, showing tobacco-stained teeth, but no sound was coming out.

His gun hand extended forward, past the housekeeper's head. His first shot buried itself in the sofa cushion, and the second in Captain Sayles's thigh. He was so determined to make his kill that he walked past me crouching in the short hall leading to the bathroom.

I moved on instinct. The air in the room was ringing with the echo of gunshots. It masked my sound. I came up behind him, grabbing his gun hand and pulling it up. At the same time, I put my foot in the back of the housekeeper, sending her sprawling to the floor. She scrambled backward, past us and out the door.

He was strong and desperate. The gun fired into the ceiling and the cabinets in the kitchenette. He got a standing leg sweep on me, and I felt myself going down. I reached out quickly, grabbing the front of his black jacket, and pulled him down with me. I twisted as I fell back to get an advantage by the time we hit the floor. Our hands, fighting over the gun, hit the corner of the wall, and the revolver went flying.

We landed side by side, and he punched me in the face two times in rapid fire. I jammed my forearm in his throat and held it there while the flashing lights of concussion cleared from my vision. He began to cough violently as he beat his fists across my arm, which was slowly compressing his larynx and supply of air.

I took this as my chance to get to my feet, but that was when he kicked backward and scrambled to find his gun.

I scrambled to the sofa, where Captain Sayles lay holding his leg, trying to staunch the bleeding. I found his service pistol on the floor next to him. I grabbed, turned, and fired blindly in the direction of the hooded man.

My shot just missed right, but it did do the job of slowing him down. He had his gun, but he still had his back to me.

"I won't fire a warning shot! The next one is in your ass!" I shouted over the ringing from all the shooting and the beating of my heart. There were voices in my earpiece, but I could barely make them out. The garage operatives and Bobby Sr. were closing in on the others who had shot into the window from the garage.

I instructed the hooded one to stay on his stomach with his hands outstretched. I shouted for David Cooley to remember he was a cop. He finally sprang from where he was hiding. Giving the hooded man a wide berth, he took the gun from just outside the hooded man's reach. I instructed David to keep it trained on him. I had to know, and I was sure David did as well.

I came up behind the hooded man. Putting my foot firmly between his shoulder blades, I reached down and pulled his winter mask off. McGill was swollen from his neck to his forehead. He hadn't shaved for some time. His ragged beard had flecks of gray in it. His eyes were red and full of venom.

## EPILOGUE

It took a twelve-hour standoff to bring Brody out of the garage. In the end, he took his own life. Ballistics on the rifle matched the bullets removed from the body of Ms. Gernst and the front edifice of Grace and Mercy Catholic Church. A subsequent search of the McGill residence produced small-caliber fragmentation shells like the ones retrieved during Butta's autopsy.

For Camp Butterfield, in exchange for giving recorded and written testimony on Brody and McGill, he would voluntarily plead guilty to mid-level racketeering charges and a sentence of four to eight years in federal prison. For Camp, it was a way to accomplish everything he needed: get Butta's killers, prove to the Colombians that he was dedicated to their cause, and get ahead of the charges that would come when McGill and Brody started telling what they knew. The way he saw it, prison time was a small price to pay for his cousin, who'd paid the ultimate price.

For the record, Officer Takeshi was cleared of any conspiracy. The plan had been to frame him or David Cooley for the death of Shawn Butterfield.

After a few days in custody, McGill was ready to talk. He was trying to save himself from the death penalty.

**Date: Friday, November 3, 2017**

**Site: Atlanta Metropolitan Police Station, #1 Protection Drive, Atlanta, GA**

**Purpose: Interrogative statement of Officer James McGill**

**RE: File 17-246117 Murder of Shawn Butterfield.**

Question: State your name and address.

McGill: James C. McGill, Officer First Class, 303 Aberdeen Circle, Bankhead.

Q: Explain the relationship between you, the deceased Officer Brody, and Marques C. Butterfield, aka Camp Butterfield.

M: This was supposed to be about Brody killing the kid.

Q: But we need to establish some precedent to give it the proper perspective. Do you want me to repeat the question?

M: No. It was like this. About five years ago, Brody and me were routinely busting Camp's street soldiers. So much so it had got to be kind of a joke.

Q: How so?

M: Either they was juveniles or first-time offenders and back on the streets in little or no time. Or they would be replaced by new ones.

Q: So, how did you come under the employ of Camp Butterfield?

M: We weren't employees. It was kind of like consultants. We had a choice to deal with him or not. We got the impression he had other cop consultants already.

Q: Let's just stick with how your arrangement worked.

M: It started off small. Just information about where he may want and not want to do business to avoid the police hassle.

Q: And you two, both decorated officers, just went along with it?

M: If you look at it from where we were standing, it was going to be money spent anyway.

Q: How so?

M: When one street soldier is arrested, and let's say it's a juvenile, there is bail, a guardian from the children's court, a spot in a children's home or foster care, maybe some counselors. Then, eventually, legal representation from a public or private defender. Now, each one of those has a fee attached to them. Butterfield was paying those fees in a lot of cases to make sure the soldier or his family kept his mouth shut.

Q: So, instead of paying all those fees?

M: He could pay us. The end result was the same. The soldier was back on the street in one or two days tops. In the beginning, Brody and I didn't even charge that much.

Q: How much did you get to start?

M: For some reason, five hundred dollars a week sounds right.

Q: Each?

M: Right, five hundred for each of us.

Q: What went wrong?

M: Just life. Life went wrong.

Q: How so?

M: The payments got bigger and better, and we got used to it. Brody had an ex-wife and three kids in Nashville. I had my own bills and a family to take care of. In-laws in assisted living facilities. Shit like that.

Q: You had political aspirations, didn't you?

M (laughing softly): Yeah, wanted to move up in the union, maybe on the national executive committee and segue into Homeland Security or National Security Administration.

Q: So, what went wrong?

M: Well, like the song says, "More money, more problems." We had to do more than find open corners for business. We had to alter evidence or lose it. We provided information on Camp's rivals.

Q: How much were you all making then?

M: You gotta understand. That was part of Camp Butterfield's success. He built loyalty by being generous. As he grew, everyone benefited.

Q: What was your share of all this growth?

M: A little over fourteen hundred dollars per week.

Q: Each?

M: Right.

Q: So, why would you spoil this by killing his cousin, who wasn't even in the business?

M (smiling): Dumbass greed. It started in Brody's mind. You gotta understand. He enjoyed the money, but he hated that it came from someone like Camp.

Q: Because Camp was a criminal?

M: Maybe, but more so because he was a criminal that was also young and black. See, Brody was always going on about how his family in Tennessee had money up until fifteen years ago. They was in construction and also had a couple of restaurants and bars. Then they lost it somehow. He always mentioned how generous his daddy and his uncles were, extending credit to poor black people. He would always say they lost the businesses from being too generous in that old-school kind of way.

Q: What did that have to do with Camp Butterfield?

M: He was young and rich beyond someone his age. Brody always hated people who came by their money too easy. That would be drug dealers, but also internet geniuses, social media sensations, and reality show stars.

Q: Go on.

M: Brody figured that he and I were doing more and more work on the street. We were picking up money and delivering to the drop houses. We knew the names of all the connects back up to the money men in Belize. We figured we might as well run it ourselves.

Q: Run what?

M: The operation.

Q: Camp's operation?

M: Right. We had seen enough of it. Once we got Camp out of the way, the Colombians could deal directly with two members of the police force. Now, that's some access for your ass.

Q: They probably would have just sent some new bosses to continue muling the both of you.

M: What?

Q: Never mind. How much of this had to do with Disciple Daniel's business?

M: What?

Q: Disciple Daniels – underground gambler, pimp. How much were you all into him?

M: That's a good question. By the time we started counting our losses, we had so much vig added to it . . .

Q: So, you just gambled all that money away.

M: Not initially. We were winning at first. Winning a lot. We started in blackjack and poker. Brody always thought he was such a hotshot player. We got in big-stakes games, and that's when we started to lose and lose big. Then we got twisted up with a couple of girls that turned out to be just shy of the legal age of consent.

Q: Then what happened?

M: We didn't sweat it that much. We said we would offer Disciple Daniels the same consultant service we did for Camp. We'd even do it for free to work off our debt.

Q: How much debt we talking about?

M: Like I said, it was hard to know the actual number because of the interest Disciple Daniels was tacking onto the debt.

Q: How much did Disciple Daniels say you owed.

M: About two hundred and fifty.

Q: Thousand?

M: Yep.

Q: Each?

M: Yep.

Q (low whistle): So, what happened when you approached Disciple Daniels with your plan?

M: He laughed at us. Said we had him confused with some small-time hood. Then, two days later, Brody and I got a visit from four of the biggest human beings I had ever seen. All with Russian accents. They basically said we needed to get that money coming back the other way or they would make an example of one of us. Said they already had contacts in the police department, and it wasn't low-level street cops.

Q: Disciple Daniels was in partnership with the Russian mob?

M: More like the Russians were hired muscle for a percentage.

Q: Then what?

M: Shiiiit, man, what do you think? We had to take over Camp's territory. The vig on that five hundred k was gaining by the week. We emptied our savings and busted some cash houses of low-level independents not associated with Camp. That bought us some time with the Russians. Then, about five Saturdays ago, we're sitting on patrol near Centennial Park, and we see this kid hauling ass down the street. At first, we think it's Camp, but why would Camp be out running in Centennial Park after eleven o'clock? We followed in the cruiser and realized it was Camp's little cousin, Shawn. He always liked dressing like Camp, but he was supposed to be in school. The kid used to handle a little street business for Camp a few years before, but he decided to go legit. We wondered if he was back at it. And if so, he was way north of Camp's territory.

Q: What did you do about it?

M: Nothing that night. We lost him north of Ivan Allen Boulevard. Then, the next Saturday, at almost the same time, here he comes again. This time, we get out ahead of him. We picked him up north of Ivan Allen Boulevard and tracked him to an apartment off Hunnicutt.

Q: This was Brianna Daniels's home?

M: No it was KiKi Daniels, a cousin. We continued to hang around. We still thought at this point that young Butta was back in the game and making a drop or a pickup. Then, five minutes after his arrival, here comes Brianna Daniels around the corner. We couldn't stick around all night. We had a few calls to respond to that night. We stayed out past our shift just to see if he was still there in the morning.

Q: And was he still there?

M: Yes, he was, but he wasn't doing business. We got the names of everyone involved, and a simple check of their Facebook pages and Instagram accounts told us all we needed. Butta and the Daniels girl were seeing each other. It was obvious that neither Camp nor Disciple Daniels knew anything about it.

Q: Ok.

M: Well, Brody and I thought about it. We didn't have the ability to outright kill Camp Butterfield. Besides, we would have to deal with that crazy Kai Davis. That butch bitch is no joke. Eventually, we needed to find a way to get Camp to trip himself up and make it look like anybody but us.

Q: You were going to kill Shawn and blame it on David Cooley.

M: There were layers to it. First was to blame it on Cooley or Takeshi, whichever one shot in the air. If that fell through, we would blame it on Disciple Daniels and his people once we told Camp about Shawn and the Daniels girl. It that didn't work, we would make attempts on whoever was accused of

Shawn's death and then blame Camp for attempts on that party's life. One of those ways, Camp would either be arrested for a revenge murder on a cop or a rival or he would be killed during the same. Either way, we didn't care.

Q: So, who shot Shawn?

M: Brody, with the long sniper rifle. We were south of the park. Cooley and Takeshi were north of the park. When Shawn passed us, Brody drove quietly north of their position to Ivan Allen Boulevard. He was already up there before Cooley arrived. He parked the cruiser on a side street and climbed on top of the yellow and black Mission Building across from Pemberton Place Pavilion, where Shawn emerged from heading north. He was there, watching Shawn as he came running through between the Coke Museum and the Georgia Aquarium. He came down the steps of the Museum of Human Rights just as Cooley was coming from his left. Brody told me by phone that things were in position, so I urged Cooley to shoot the warning shot at that moment. It was a narrow window for the plan to work.

Q: How did Brady sync his shot to Cooley's?

M: By the sound. He had Shawn in his scope. When he heard Cooley's shot, he fired. It was close enough.

Q: Camp was slow to respond.

M (chuckling): Fucking Camp always was careful, very careful. I guess that's why him and Kai lasted so long. It didn't help that Cooley was a damn boy scout, all kinds of awards for working with kids and old folks.

Q: That was when you set out to frame him by going after

Cooley and his family.

M: Yeah, I thought we still had time. We were urging Cooley to take a plea deal. At the same time, we were urging Camp not to waste time. If we killed Cooley or his family, we would make sure Camp was blamed for it. The Russians were getting impatient. Brody was getting scared, talking about running.

Q: And the night at the hotel?

M: Well, that was a trap, right? We thought the Russians were applying pressure, but it was just Disciple Daniels telling us that the Russians were getting impatient. That's why we never suspected the hotel for being a bad setup. What can I say? We were getting desperate.

Q: Did you know the Daniels girl was pregnant by Shawn?

M: Yeah, we overheard that Paladin Security guy reporting to Captain Sayles. He seemed to be around the case a lot, looking back on it, but it didn't register at the time. We thought the pregnancy would throw suspicion on Disciple Daniels.

Q: What happened?

M: In the end, we presented too many possibilities, and Camp ended up not biting on any of it. Then all the parties started talking to each other. Is it true that Camp got a sit-down with Cooley? That's how he found out we were with him that night.

Q: Not sure. Anything else?

M: Naw, I just wish I would never have met Camp Butterfield.

He ruined my life.

**End of Statement**

James McGill was sentenced to fifteen to twenty years in federal prison. They made sure to assign him to a different facility than Camp Butterfield. In the end, it made no difference. McGill choked to death during dinner one night at the federal detainment center just days before he was to be transported to his final facility. The food got stuck in his throat and expanded to the point that it prevented his ability to swallow.


David Cooley was reinstated in the Metro Police Department, but he soon left to take a job in a police department in Suwannee, Georgia. He never told Anousha that he knew Camp Butterfield was the guy she'd been seeing behind his back. He had seen her with the guy back when they'd been separated, but it had just been a side glance. He'd never seen his face. Then, during that meeting in the safe house, there had been an obvious intimacy. Plus, he'd used the house nickname for her and the baby. He'd even looked at Camp Butterfield from behind and known it was the same guy. In the end, he didn't care. He just wanted to disappear from the world with his little family.

I returned to St. Louis with the team. The next day, I went to see my mother and gave her the report I knew she wanted but would never force me to do. In the end, I felt more whole than I had in over a year. My phone was full of messages from TruLuv and Lola. The three of us had our own little group text club. I never erased them. TruLuv was doing an

HBU tour. Lola and Tommi B. were such a hit that they were asked to perform as part of the lineup at food and wine festivals at all six Disney parks. We were making plans to go on vacation during the holidays. If not then, then definitely by the first quarter of the new year.

The End